KISSING BY THE MISTLETOE

by Cora Lee

This is a work of fiction. Names, characters, businesses, places, events, and incidents are either the products of the author's imagination or used in a fictitious manner.

Editing by Jude Simms

ISBN 978-1-944477-28-8

Published in the United States by More Than Words Press

For the Sweet Summer Kisses ladies who gave me my first opportunity to become a published author: Erin, Aileen, Heather, Marie, Lily, Elizabeth, Bess, and Susana. I wouldn't be where I am without you!

Chapter 1

Kent, England
December 1813

MADDIE HAYWARD PERCHED ON THE edge of her chair in Mrs. Spencer's drawing room, back straight, dark hair neatly pinned up, politely smiling as she sipped from a tea cup painted with delicate pink and yellow flowers.

"I understand the Mathisons will be visiting your family for a few weeks," Mrs. Spencer announced.

The other ladies in the room tittered and Maddie fought to keep her smile from slipping. "That's right."

"Mrs. Mathison and...both her sons?" someone else asked, not quite able to sound nonchalant.

Maddie suppressed the urge to roll her eyes. Kit Mathison, the oldest son, had been Maddie's best friend for years—since before his father died and his mother had taken her children to Edinburgh, where her brother lived. Because Kit was handsome, unattached, and possessed a comfortable income, Maddie was supposed to be in love with him.

She did love him, but as the brother she never had, not as a potential husband. Yet whenever she corrected people's assumptions, her words were dismissed. Apparently no one could conceive of a gentleman and a lady maintaining a close friendship without designs on each other.

"Yes," Maddie responded, hoping no one else heard the slight edge in her voice. "Kit and Thomas will both be accompanying their mother."

"You're so lucky," a younger woman sighed. "How wonderful would it be to dance with Kit Mathison?"

Maddie smiled at that with genuine goodwill. Dancing with the local women was something Kit had mentioned in his last letter. It was one of the things he was most looking forward to. "Perhaps you'll have the chance at the assembly this week. I know for a fact that he's eager to see everyone."

Mrs. Spencer waved her hand reprovingly, but let out a little chuckle. "Miss Hayward, you shouldn't tease. We are all aware to whom Mr. Mathison will be directing his attention."

And there was the other side of the coin —Kit was also reputed to be in love with Maddie.

For his part, Kit was highly amused by the whole situation. The consequences were less severe for him, though. Ladies still swooned over him, and not one would decline his addresses. Maddie, being female, was at a disadvantage: she was supposed to try to attract a gentleman and wait for him to initiate a courtship. But no true gentleman would encroach on what he saw as another man's dominion.

Which left Maddie in a precarious position. She had few practical skills, no wealthy family, and little money of her own. If she failed to marry, her only option was to remain in her parents' home and find some way to contribute to the household, lest she become a burden to them.

She smiled as best she could at Mrs. Spencer, feeling her resistance fade away. There wasn't any use in arguing when no one listened to the argument. "But he can't be by my side all the time."

With Maddie's seeming acceptance of the situation, the ladies of the drawing room beamed at her. Then they changed the subject, and no one spoke to Maddie directly for the rest of the visit.

"How does Mrs. Spencer?" Maddie's

mother asked when she returned home. "Did she carry on about her new teacups the way I thought she would?"

"She looked well," Maddie answered, removing her bonnet and smoothing down her hair. "She was very keen on the new teacups, yes, but they weren't the focus of our conversation."

Her mother grinned. "I'm sure I know what was, though. How many ladies asked after Kit?"

This time Maddie let her eyes roll. Not that she didn't expect it from her mother, but she'd been hoping they might get through one day without an allusion to her supposed relationship with Kit.

Apparently it wasn't this day. "They all did, at one point or another."

"You are a lucky girl," her mother said, echoing the sentiments of the drawing room ladies. "To think, in just a few weeks' time you could be Mrs. Christopher Mathison."

"What?"

"Surely he'll make you a pretty proposal at Christmas, with both families here to celebrate."

Maddie's mother was practically glowing at the thought of her daughter marrying the head of the Mathison family. Misplaced though it was, Maddie didn't have the heart to shatter the illusion. Everyone would settle down again when Christmas came and went with no proposal of marriage from Kit. And if she truly was lucky, he would find the right woman and marry her. Quickly.

She kissed her mother's cheek and headed to her bedchamber, putting her bonnet in its usual place in her battered wardrobe. What if Kit didn't marry quickly? How long could she linger with the wallflowers and chaperones at every event, unseen by gentlemen who might otherwise have taken an interest in her?

What if he didn't marry at all?

The thought nearly knocked the breath out of her. All Maddie had ever wanted was to have a home and children of her own, to share her life with a man she adored. If Kit remained unattached, would everyone continue to think of her as his? Would she slip into spinsterhood while the eligible bachelors of Kent looked elsewhere?

Maddie dropped onto her bed, bracing her hands against the pomegranate red counterpane her grandmother had brought with her from Spain when she'd married Maddie's grandfather. What would she have done in this situation?

Maddie laid back and grinned. Gran would have flouted convention and begun asking gentlemen to dance and drive and walk out with her. Maddie wasn't quite so bold, but perhaps there was something she could do to take control of her life—this aspect of it, at least. Perhaps Kit would have some ideas, or maybe his brother, Thomas, could help.

She pictured Thomas as she'd last seen him, tall and lanky, his reddish hair curling every which way when he didn't try to tame it with pomade. That had been the last time he'd visited the Haywards, right before he went off to university three years ago. He'd always been kind to her, quick to offer a helping hand when she'd needed one.

Of course, she'd only ever needed his assistance exiting a carriage or his company walking into the village. But Thomas was clever. If he and Kit and Maddie put their heads together, she was certain they'd come up with some way to uncouple her from Kit's non-existent romantic attachment.

Thomas Mathison sat on the rear-facing seat in his brother's traveling coach, his eyes drifting out the window to watch the scenery roll past as he wiped his palms on his trousers. He'd been looking forward to this visit since Mrs. Hayward proposed the idea two months ago, but the closer they drew to the Haywards' home, the more frenzied the butterflies in his stomach became. He had corresponded some with Maddie in the years since they'd last seen each other, so it wasn't as if they'd be strangers after so much time apart. But what if things had changed for her that she hadn't mentioned in her letters? Was she still interested in gardening? Still fleet of foot when skating on the little pond near the village?

An image of ice skating with Maddie formed in his mind, as clear as if it had happened only moments ago: Maddie skating backward, bundled up against the cold, holding Thomas's hands as he drew her closer with promises to keep her warm. She wrapped her arms around his neck and lifted her face for his kiss, and he obliged with a grin.

One of the carriage wheels rolled over a rock and Thomas's head bumped against the window, dissolving the image. Maddie undoubtedly thought of him as Kit's little brother and nothing else. Perhaps she was even skating with—and being warmed by—someone else, even as the geographical gap between them was closing. The thought pierced his heart and he had to stifle a grunt of pain.

Not that he had any claim on her. He had thought it prudent to wait until he'd found work and saved up enough money to support a wife before he spoke to Maddie of love and marriage. He smoothed his hands over his thighs, attempting to wipe away the sweat that was forming again on his palms. Maybe it would be better if Maddie found someone else, someone who wouldn't have to worry about whether or not he could afford a home and clothing and food for more than just himself. She deserved to be with a man who could take care of her, who could give her not only the things she needed but everything she wanted.

"Thomas, dear, are you all right?"

He turned to his mother, sitting

opposite him, and blinked. "Yes, I'm quite well."

"Are you certain? It sounded as though you'd hit your head rather hard."

He heard a quiet chuckle from Kit's side of the carriage. "Don't worry mother. Thomas's head is hard enough to withstand a little bump."

Thomas smirked at his brother. "Not as hard as yours, of course. Didn't you once get hit by a mallet and keep right on walking?" Thomas knew very well about the mallet—he'd been holding it when it had bashed Kit in the temple. Accidentally, of course.

Kit grinned and rapped his knuckles against his skull. "Sturdy as a block of marble."

"I do hope the two of you won't be acting like adolescents in the presence of the Haywards," their mother sighed. "Maddie Hayward will not look fondly on a man who cannot put his boyhood behind him."

Kit laughed. "Maddie is the one who gave Thomas the mallet, Mother."

Their mother pressed her lips together for a moment before saying, "Yes, but that was years ago. I'm sure she's become a well-behaved young lady now, and if you want to pay your addresses to her, you ought to consider your own behavior."

It was a common refrain among the Mathisons, that Kit and Maddie would settle down together someday. No one but Kit knew of the hope Thomas harbored regarding Maddie, and that was the way he preferred it. But it still stung to have that hope so easily dashed by his own mother.

"I will promise to behave myself," Kit said, patting his mother's hand as it lay on the seat between them. "But I will not promise to court Maddie, no matter how many times you imply that I want to."

"There's no harm in wanting to spend time with her again before you ask for her hand," their mother smiled. "But you can't have been so close to her all these years without meaning to marry her."

"I can, Mother. And I have."

"What about me?" Thomas blurted out. "I've been close to her, too. Might it be possible that I want to marry her?"

He could feel his cheeks warming, and hoped he wasn't actually blushing. His mother was studying his face as if he might be, but then she shook her head.

"Your relationship with her isn't like Kit's. I know that you're fond of her, but she has always spent more time with your brother. She confides in him."

Thomas knew that was true, but felt himself frowning nonetheless. "You don't think Maddie could ever be interested in me?"

His mother reached across the carriage and took his hand for a moment. "I know that there are several ladies in Edinburgh who have already set their caps for you, my sweet boy—your uncle has told me as much. You've been the toast of his social circle since you arrived, he said, and you'll have scores of women to choose from when you're ready to take a wife."

Thomas could see the pride in her eyes, in the set of her mouth, and it warmed him.

"But," she went on, "Maddie was meant for Kit."

Kit crossed his arms over his chest with a frown, but didn't protest. Thomas wasn't surprised—the family joke about hard-headedness didn't just apply to the two brothers. Their mother could be absolutely single-minded when it came to certain subjects, and arguing with her was often a fruitless occupation.

He went back to his window, noting the addition of a few darker clouds among the puffy white ones. He came back to the idea that it might be better if Maddie did have a beau. That would leave Kit free of their mother's expectations and allow Thomas to put aside a dream that would likely never come true. He'd only have to deal with the pain of seeing her with someone else for a few weeks, then he could get on with the business of living without her. One day, he might even find contentment with one of the ladies his mother had mentioned.

Yes, that would be the easiest way out of this dilemma. He would simply ignore the possibility of impending heartbreak.

Chapter 2

Maddie had tried to stay awake long enough to greet the Mathisons when they arrived, but she'd fallen asleep before their carriage had pulled into the drive. Breakfast the following morning was her first chance to see her old friends and she fairly bounced down the stairs.

A wide variety of foods had been laid out on the sideboard and Thomas was the only person seated at the table, reading her father's weeks-old newspaper, when Maddie entered the dining room.

"Good morning."

He glanced up from the newspaper and

clambered to his feet when recognition dawned. "Miss Hayward."

She shut the door behind her and crossed the room, holding her hands out to him. "So formal," she replied with mock solemnity. "You'd never know we once fished barefoot together in the brook."

His large hands were cold when he clasped hers, but he grinned. "It was more than once, if I recall correctly. And Kit was put out the last time because you caught the biggest fish."

Maddie laughed at the memory. "Yes he was. He didn't speak to me for two whole days after that. Fortunately, you were nice enough to keep me company until he came to terms with my fishing abilities."

"It was a lovely, *quiet* two days," Thomas quipped, dropping a kiss on each of her hands before releasing them to pull out a chair for her.

"Is that what you're hoping for during this visit?" she asked, settling onto the hard wooden chair. "Peace and quiet?"

He seated himself and propped his elbow on the table, resting his chin on his palm. "Some." His blue eyes shifted to the cream and pale blue wallpaper behind her. "Edinburgh is lovely, and my uncle has made me feel very welcome. But I miss the serenity of the country."

"Does that mean you won't be attending the assembly in the village this evening?" Disappointment filtered through her at the thought.

His gaze moved back to her, but she couldn't read his expression. Was that a half smile on his lips or a grimace? "Yes, I'll be attending. It's been a while since I've danced, but I am looking forward to doing so."

"I'm sure the local ladies are looking forward to partnering you, too." She winked, slouching back against her chair for a moment as an idea formed in her mind. "Would you, perhaps, want to dance with me tonight? Just once," she added hastily, straightening again and regretting her sudden burst of daring. She'd put Thomas in the awkward position of having to dance with her or risk hurting her feelings, and she knew he'd choose her comfort over his own if pressed. "I wouldn't want to keep you from your adoring public."

His brows rose for a blink-and-you'd-miss-it moment, then his lids dropped and his mouth curved into a smile. "I think the adoring public will be more interested in Kit than me. But I would be honored to dance with you, Maddie. As often as you like."

His eyes met hers as he spoke the last phrase, and she felt...*something*. She broke contact before she could inspect the feeling too closely, and pushed back her chair.

Thomas was on his feet in one graceful movement before she could fully get to hers. "May I fix you a plate?"

Maddie rose and pushed in her chair, touching her fingertips to his shoulders—broader and more muscled than she remembered—as she passed him on the way to the sideboard. "Thank you, but I can manage on my own. Can I fix you a plate while I'm up? Or are you content with tea this morning?"

"You can fix me a plate," a voice boomed as the door swung open.

"Kit!" Maddie changed course and headed for the door, arriving there just in time to be engulfed in Kit's brawny arms. "I thought you'd be sleeping late this morning."

"Not me," he laughed, releasing her. "I prefer to keep country hours, just as Thomas prefers to keep clerk's hours, even when he is not on duty."

Kit winked at his brother, following Maddie to the sideboard and filling a plate for himself.

"Good morning to you, too, brother," Thomas responded mildly.

Kit grinned and carried his and Maddie's plates to the table when they'd made their selections, settling in beside her. "I'm going over to the old house this afternoon if the snow holds off. Would the two of you care to accompany me?"

Maddie returned his grin. At five-and-twenty, Kit was finally old enough to take possession of his inheritance, according to the terms of his father's will. He'd spoken of little else in his last few letters, anxious to re-open the house in which he and Thomas had spent their boyhood. "How exciting! I would love nothing more than to go with you, but I'm afraid my mother won't allow it. I'm to rest today, so I won't look tired at the assembly tonight."

"You'll look lovely whether you 'rest' today or not," Kit scoffed. "Won't she, brother?"

Was it her imagination, or were Thomas's cheeks turning the faintest shade of pink? "Of course," he answered, his voice slightly gruff.

Maddie felt her own cheeks warm unexpectedly. Kit had complimented her more times than she could remember, and certainly with more enthusiasm—why did this bland remark from Thomas provoke such a reaction?

"Thank you both." She picked up her fork and focused on her breakfast, brushing away the thought. "But as long as I reside with my parents, I must comply with their wishes. I expect you boys will have a grand time reliving your past, though. And making plans for the future."

With any luck, Kit's plans would involve finding a wife and Maddie would be free to find her own happiness. What would Thomas do? He had begun working for his uncle, who was a barrister in Edinburgh, after finishing university—did he plan to do so always? Did he hope to strike out on his own some day? Did he, too, plan to marry?

Maddie was surprised to discover she didn't know. She was even more surprised to discover that she wanted to know, though that revelation shouldn't have been so shocking. Thomas was her best friend's brother, and her friend in his own right. It made perfect sense that she'd be curious about his wishes and goals.

"As long as we return in time to go to the assembly," Thomas said, smiling gently at Maddie. "I have a promise to keep."

"Come, brother, we must be getting back."

Thomas acknowledged Kit's words with an absent nod. He was staring into the frozen brook that cut across the property—the same brook Maddie had pulled her ire-inducing fish from—purposefully delaying their return. He was nervous about dancing with her, even though he'd never been so before. What if he tripped over his own feet? What if he stepped on hers and crushed her toes? What if she had only asked him for a dance to be polite?

"Yes, of course," he replied, tearing his gaze from the ice and heading toward the stable with Kit.

They readied their horses in relative

silence, but once they were both in the saddle and on their way back to the Haywards' home, Kit got chatty.

"You've promised Maddie a dance this evening, have you?"

"I have," Thomas said as matter-of-factly as he was able.

"She told me after you'd gone in search of your boots."

Of course she had. She told Kit everything. "Did she also mention that she asked me for the dance?"

Kit nodded, pulling his beaver hat down lower over his ears. "Yes. She's afraid only we will pay her any attention and she'll be stuck sitting with the matrons and wallflowers all evening." He paused, throwing Thomas a pointed look. "This could be your chance."

"Chance for what?" Thomas hoped his brother would change the subject if he played dumb. It wasn't that he didn't want to talk about Maddie, but the more they discussed her, the more he let himself imagine a future with her.

"Your chance with Maddie, you dolt," Kit chuckled. "She's asked me to stay away for most of the evening in the hopes other men would speak with her."

"Am I 'other men'?"

"You certainly could be. And you've already secured a dance with her."

Thomas licked his dry lips. "It's just a dance, Kit."

"And that is how many happy courtships have begun."

The wind picked up, blowing frigid air down from the north and requiring them both to pull their scarves up over their faces, which halted any further conversation. Thomas was grateful for it, and for his brother's silence on the subject of Maddie once they'd returned to the Hayward house with just enough time to ready themselves for the evening.

The families took two separate carriages to the Flying Horse Inn, the tallest building in the village and the only place with a room large enough for a gathering of so many people. Once they were all together in the dooryard, Mr. Hayward offered his arm to his wife.

"Shall we?"

She smiled and laid her hand on the sleeve of his coat. "By all means."

Thomas turned to his mother, about to make her the same offer, when Kit swooped in and beat him to it.

"This way, Mother," he said, glancing at Thomas for the briefest of moments.

That left Maddie standing alone.

"May I escort you in?" Thomas asked, hoping his voice didn't sound as hesitant to her as it did to him.

It was dark, but her brown eyes were sparkling in the light of the carriage lanterns. "You may."

He'd expected her to formally place her hand on his sleeve, as was the custom. But instead she threaded her arm through his and rested her hand on his biceps. It was likely for show, but it was an intimate gesture all the same and Thomas had to remind himself that tonight was a favor for Maddie, not a prelude to something more.

He had to remind himself again once they were inside to counter his brother's words ringing in his ears. Thomas helped her remove her winter cloak, revealing a wine-colored gown with tiny ruffles along the sleeves and neckline. The rest of the gown was unadorned—some might even call it plain—but she needed nothing else to take his breath.

She glanced at him over her shoulder, then turned her body to face him. "What?"

His eyes widened. Had he gasped aloud? "You, erm, you look beautiful. That color suits you."

"Thank you." She poked a finger into his chest as he shed his greatcoat. "It looks well on you, too."

Thomas's eyes followed her finger and he grinned. Under his chocolate brown cutaway coat, he'd worn a cream waistcoat embroidered in claret red roses. "We're a match.”

The words were barely out of his mouth before he realized the double meaning and clamped his mouth shut. Fortunately, Maddie didn't seem to notice and Thomas allowed a small sigh to escape his lips, of both relief and frustration. Was this how he was going to spend the entire evening? Tripping all over himself around Maddie, then chastising himself for it?

No, he wasn't. He was going to enjoy himself and relish a dance with the woman he loved. Tomorrow morning their relationship would return to its previous state, and in a few weeks' time he would be on his way back to Scotland.

“Are you well, Thomas?”

Maddie's words snapped him out of his woolgathering and he nodded. “I was wondering if it might be best to have our dance first or if we should wait a little.”

“First,” she said resolutely. “The sooner I'm seen with someone other than Kit, the better. And,” her pink lips pulled into a smile, "I have been told the first dance is to be a minuet."

"You like minuets?" They were old fashioned and falling out of favor with the younger generation. Thomas couldn't remember the last time he'd danced one.

Her lashes swept down as her gaze dropped for a moment. "They make me feel rather stately and elegant," she confessed in a low voice, leaning close enough for Thomas to notice she'd chosen a different scent for the evening—roses. "Something I tend not to be otherwise."

He bent his head to speak softly in her ear as he offered her his hand. "Then let's go and be elegant."

She took his hand and allowed him to lead her onto the dance floor, a slow smile spreading across her face that sent his heart off at a gallop. The small orchestra began to play and Thomas moved through the steps of the dance with Maddie, to-ing and fro-ing, parting and coming together again. They both wore gloves with their evening wear, of course, but he cataloged every handclasp, every brush of shoulders, every accidental touch so that he might recall them all when he'd returned to his life in Edinburgh. If he could never afford to ask Maddie for her hand in marriage, he would at least remember this dance with her.

The song came to an end and another gentleman approached to ask Maddie for a dance. Thomas bowed and slid away into the crowd, trying with little success to keep from turning and watching her. She moved through the dance with a lightness not so much of body—she managed the steps as one who had practiced them often but not necessarily with any great love for the action—but with a lightness of spirit. His own heart lifted and found himself smiling. He made for the refreshment table, hoping to find himself a cup of good, strong punch to further the warm feeling that had begun to grow in his chest. The music changed once again and Thomas turned back one last time, catching a glimpse of Maddie laughing with delight as she hopped her way through a Scotch reel. Good. Her plan had worked, then, and he'd have memories of her to cherish always.

Chapter 3

THE HAYWARDS AND MATHISONS GATHERED in the Hayward parlor the next afternoon, whiling away the gray day in relative quiet and comfort. Mr. Hayward was sprawled in a chair reading the newspaper, Kit was writing letters at the small desk in the corner, and Mrs. Mathison and Mrs. Hayward were working out of their sewing baskets by the fire with Maddie, whose eyes kept drifting toward the window opposite her.

Thomas tried to focus on the book he was holding, but *The Philosophy of Nature, or, the Influence of Scenery on the Mind and Heart* just wasn't capturing his attention.

"Maddie, would you like to take a walk with me?" he asked across the small room. "I know it's cold outside…"

"Yes," she answered quickly. "I believe I could use some fresh air."

There were the usual appeals from the parents to dress warmly, which they both heeded, wearing heavy boots, thick stockings, and extra layers beneath their long coats when they met at the door. They left the house and walked along in silence for a dozen yards, not touching but not actively avoiding one another either.

"I'm so glad you asked me to walk with you," Maddie finally said, her breath puffing out before her in a small cloud. "I wanted to thank you for last night. For the first time in over a year I danced with two other gentlemen, and had an entire conversation where Kit wasn't even mentioned. All thanks to you."

He'd tried to ignore her dancing partners last night—both well-dressed gentlemen with tolerable manners—but had been unable to ignore the luminous smile she'd worn all evening. He'd have run into a burning building to see that smile, but it hadn't been for him. "I'm glad you enjoyed yourself," he said softly, sincerely. "And that I could be of service."

They walked along for a few more minutes without speaking before he felt her mittened hand on his arm. "I— I don't want to impose, but might I ask another favor of you?"

"Of course," he answered without hesitation. If there was any earthly thing he could do to make her happy, he would certainly do it.

"Would you, perhaps... We're all going to the Duke of Alston's Midwinter Fête a few days hence, and I thought you might..."

Ah. No dancing during this outing, but he could see where she was going. "Might like to escort you? While Kit keeps out of the way, of course."

He said the last with a bit of cheek and

she laughed nervously, clasping her hands together at her waist. "I know it's a lot to ask…"

Thomas stopped and reached for her hands, bringing her to a gentle halt before him. "You know Kit would do anything to secure your happiness." He squeezed her hands, wishing for a moment that they were indoors again with no need of mittens. "As would I."

"Truly?"

"Always."

She took a small step closer to him, dropping her gaze to the snow beneath their feet for a moment. "Then might I impose upon you for the length of your stay here?"

He pressed his lips together and raised his brows, trying to discern her meaning. "You want me to escort you instead of Kit…until I depart?"

"More than that," she said, tipping her head back to meet his gaze. "I would like you to pretend to court me until you depart so people will know I'm not betrothed to Kit."

She was trembling now, and Thomas tried to resist the urge to pull her against him. "You're freezing," he said instead. "We should go back inside and warm you up."

Maddie shook her head. "I'm not cold. But I might be slightly terrified."

"Of me?"

"Of what you must think of me for being so forward," she said, releasing his hands and wrapping her arms around herself. "And of what your answer will be."

He glanced around and, noting a copse of pines a few feet away, drew her among them, out of the wind and away from any prying eyes that might be about. "Might *I* be forward for a moment? You look as though you need to be held, and I would like to oblige you."

She went into his arms without another word, pressing her cheek against his coat and holding on to him like a drowning woman to a raft. Her trembling ceased a few moments later, and Thomas felt his own muscles relax as he rested his chin on the top of her head. It was a relief and a boon to be able to offer her comfort, and the embrace gave him time to contemplate her request.

"Better?"

He felt her chest expand against him as she breathed deeply in, then contract again when she exhaled slowly. "Yes. Thank you. I don't know what came over me..."

"You're stuck in an undesirable situation, and need help getting out of it," he said, palming her cheek for the briefest of touches. "I might react the same way in your place."

"I doubt it." She pulled back and offered him a slight smile. "But thank you for saying so. I just— I am also more than slightly terrified that I'll never find a husband. Which I'm sure sounds silly to you."

"Not at all," he said. And it didn't. He knew what society thought of women who eschewed matrimony, regardless of the reason. He also knew how much more independence she'd have as a married woman with the right husband. She'd have a home and possibly children of her own, but she'd also have the freedom to go about in public without anyone else's permission—independence she would never be allowed as a spinster daughter still living with her parents. "I didn't realize Kit's presence loomed so large."

She blew out a breath and took another half step backward, still within the circle of his arms but apart from him at the same time. "It does, even more so now that he's come to claim his inheritance. Eligible men won't even look at me. All they see is Kit's intended."

"But if someone else is courting you, the illusion of your impending marriage to Kit is shattered."

"Exactly." She slid her hands down his arms, clasping his fingers in hers. "There is no one else I can ask to do this, Thomas.

But I don't want you to feel pressured into agreeing. If you are uncomfortable with this idea, you may tell me so and there will be no hard feelings."

She might not want him to feel pressured, yet he did all the same. The pressure wasn't coming from Maddie, though—it came from himself. Certainly he wanted to do everything in his power to make her happy. Did that include inducing his own insanity? For him there would be no pretending. Anytime he touched her, looked at her, caught the scent of gardenias she often wore, he would look for all the world like a man in love because he would be one. Then he'd have to forget anything had ever happened and hie himself back to Edinburgh, while she made a life with another man.

Could he do it?

He looked down into her dark eyes and saw hope mingling with fear. If he said no, she'd remain in social limbo as Kit's future wife without actually being Kit's future wife.

But if he said yes he would be giving her a measure of control back. And she would be his, even if only for a few weeks.

"Have you spoken to Kit about this plan?"

"No. This is your decision alone. I came to you first."

So there truly was no outside pressure. No one would ever know if he refused her.

But he would know. "I said that I would do anything to secure your happiness. If a beau for Christmas is what you need, than that is what I shall be."

"You're going to do what?"

Maddie stood with Thomas in the bedchamber he shared with his brother. Thomas wasn't touching her, but his presence beside her was enough to bolster her courage.

"Thomas and I are going to have a faux

courtship," she repeated, meeting Kit's gaze with determination. "And we need you to play along."

"You're to play this game until Thomas returns to Scotland after the New Year?"

"Yes."

Kit's brow wrinkled. "Won't people just go back to assuming you and I are betrothed?"

That was a legitimate concern, particularly with Kit remaining at his childhood home not two miles away.

"Not if someone takes an interest in her before my departure," Thomas said.

Kit raised a blond eyebrow at that, but it quickly returned to its usual place. "So I am to stay away from you in public, and I can't spend any time with you alone during our visit."

"I know it isn't ideal," Maddie told him. "I've missed you, and we haven't really spent much time together since your arrival. But if we maintain a public distance, even around our parents, then I may finally have a suitor—a chance at a life of my own."

Kit's eyes flicked from Maddie to Thomas, then back again. "And you've agreed to this, brother?"

"I have."

Maddie smiled at his declaration. She had no idea how she'd ever repay Thomas for his cooperation in this scheme, but she would spend the rest of her days finding a way.

"All right, then. I'll play my part as well." Kit rose from the bed where he'd been sitting and grinned. "I suppose that means we won't be playing skittles together this year, then."

Maddie laughed. They had a rivalry in that sport that stretched back to their first Midwinter Fête as children, and this year was a tie-breaking year. "I'm afraid not."

"Perhaps Thomas will take up the Mathison mantle on my behalf, then." Kit winked at his brother. "Keep the tradition going."

"I'll do my best," Thomas grinned.

The three of them played their assigned parts over the next few days: Kit remaining friendly but never alone with Maddie, Thomas becoming more attentive to her, taking her aside from time to time for a private conversation when their parents were about, and Maddie herself pretending she didn't miss the closeness she had with Kit even as she enjoyed spending more time with Thomas.

By the time the two families arrived at the Duke of Alston's estate for the Midwinter Fête, it was becoming second nature for Maddie to take Thomas's arm and walk with him as if they'd been courting for months.

"Where would you like to go first?" he asked, as their various family members scattered in different directions.

Maddie looked around at the booths and tents that stretched off into the distance. "That way." She pointed to her left, where a booth sat with cakes decorating every horizontal surface. "I can smell the warm cinnamon from here. Perhaps they have Chelsea buns."

"Excellent idea."

They had only made it halfway to their destination, though, when they came upon a crying child. Dressed all in gray wool, he looked to be a boy of perhaps five years old with tears pouring down his cheeks.

Maddie knelt down in the snow, heedless of the cold that immediately began to soak into her own clothing. "Whatever is the matter?" she asked softly.

"I can't find my brother," the child wailed, rubbing his eyes.

Maddie tried to smile reassuringly, thumbing tears off his cheeks. "Maybe we can help you find him."

She turned and shot a questioning look up at Thomas, who dropped to one knee beside her. "I'm certain we can. If I put you up on my shoulders, you'll be taller than everyone here. I'd wager you'd be able to see your brother then."

The boy turned wide eyes on Thomas. "Taller than everyone?"

Thomas nodded solemnly and Maddie felt her heart swell. Many men were awkward with children, but Thomas's manner with the little boy was as easy as if they'd always been friends.

"Yes," Thomas said. "Would you like to try?"

The boy sniffled, but nodded.

"Here, I'll lift you up," Maddie offered, reaching for the child as Thomas sank down onto his haunches. She scooped the boy up and hefted him onto Thomas's shoulders, bracing him until Thomas had a firm hold on him.

Thomas rose to his feet slowly and turned to her. "Where should we start, do you think?"

She choked back a laugh. The boy had his little arms wrapped around the crown of Thomas's head, and Thomas carried on as if the situation was perfectly normal. "Where was the last place you saw your brother?" she called up to the boy.

"By the toys," he answered, knocking Thomas's hat off and leaning down into his curly hair.

"By the toys," Thomas echoed resolutely, smiling at Maddie when she scooped up his hat and handed it back to him. "Let's try there first." He held his hat in one hand and reached out the other to Maddie, which she took with a grin she couldn't smother.

Her grin did fade a bit after nearly thirty minutes of searching. But the child finally spotted his missing brother near the bonfire burning at the edge of the festivities. The brother, they discovered, had gone to procure food for the both of them, confident that his youngest sibling was following along behind...until he'd turned to find the boy wasn't behind him at all.

Thomas hoisted the child up and over his head, setting him down on the ground. "You stick close to your brother for the rest of the night, now," he said, his tone serious but amiable.

"Yes sir."

"But if you do lose him again, we'll help you find him."

The boy smiled brightly. "Thank you!"

He scurried off with his older brother, and Maddie clasped Thomas's hand in both of hers. "That is possibly the sweetest thing I have ever seen."

"The boy? He was rather cute, wasn't he?"

She laughed, leaning in to rest her head against his shoulder. She shouldn't have with all the people swirling around them, but it was less scandalous than throwing her arms around him the way she wanted to.

"The pair of you," she clarified. "You're a natural with children."

He smiled down at her for a long moment. "I do hope to have some of my own one day."

An image popped into her head of

Thomas leading a cluster of redheaded children to a brook for a day of fishing, of a tender Thomas bending to instruct the little ones how to hold a rod, smiling over their heads at their unseen mother.

"You'll make a marvelous father when the time comes," she said, pushing the thought from her mind.

"I hope so." He was quiet for a spell, adjusting his grip on her hands but never releasing them. Then, "Do you want children, Maddie?"

Children with curly auburn hair and blue eyes like their father? She gave herself a mental shake. "Erm, yes, I do. Someday."

But, she reminded herself, not with Thomas. He had a life to return to that didn't include her, and she had a future husband out there somewhere waiting to be found.

"Well, we still have some of the evening left to ourselves." She forced her mouth into a smile to cover the abrupt change in subject. "What should we do next?"

Chapter 4

MADDIE SPENT THE NEXT TWO days trapped with too many people inside a house that felt too small. For the first time in her life she ached for some time alone but absolutely none was forthcoming. Is this what it would be like as she grew older yet remained at home? Her parents' presence becoming more and more confining? Her total dependence upon them flung in her face at every turn?

A break finally arrived when her parents and Mrs. Mathison took themselves off to bed early one night after dinner, leaving her alone with Kit and Thomas in the parlor.

"You know they're all hoping I'll go to bed, too," Thomas said, glancing from Kit to Maddie.

"Then they will be sorely disappointed," she returned with more hope in her voice than she'd intended to show. "Won't they?"

Kit rose and stretched. "Do you think they'll be disappointed if *I* go to bed? I spent the day climbing around on a roof attempting a repair, and all I want to do is sleep."

"Go to bed," Maddie said, shooing him out the door. "I want to hear all about the work you've been doing on the house, but it will keep until tomorrow."

"You two can discuss the next stage of your plan without my interfering," he grinned. "Good night."

When he'd gone and shut the door behind him, Thomas stood and stretched as well.

"Are you going to leave me, too?"

Maddie was unsure how she felt about the idea. She'd finally be alone if Thomas retired for the evening, but the idea no longer held the same appeal.

"Never." He seated himself on the floor before the fire with a small smile. "That is, unless you want me to."

She returned his smile from her place on the sofa, set at a right angle to the fireplace. "I can't imagine ever wanting that."

Maddie could have sworn the expression on his face wavered into something darker, but it disappeared before she could properly identify the emotion behind it.

"Once upon a time, you would have done anything to get rid of me," he chuckled. "The irritating little brother trailing along behind you and Kit."

"You weren't irritating. A little annoying on occasion," she teased, leaning over the arm of the sofa, "especially with that old green cape you used to wear everywhere...even in the summertime. Where on earth did you find that thing, anyway?"

He laughed, kicking his long legs out before him. "It was in some discarded trunk in the attic, I think. I never found out who it had belonged to, but wearing it made me feel older—old enough to tag along after my big brother, anyway."

"You're not tagging along after him anymore, though," she said softly. "You've forged your own path in life while Kit goes on with his."

"I've started on my path," he amended. "I still have some way to go before I'll feel secure on it."

"Do you think you'll ever feel secure? Truly secure?" What would it be like to have control over her own future the way a man did?

"I hope so." He turned to look at her fully, raising one knee and resting an arm on it. "What about you?"

She planted an elbow on the sofa's arm

and dropped her chin into her hand. "I don't know," Her words were slow even as her mind whirled. The dimly lit room and his confession about the cape made her want to tell some of her own secrets, but the idea was both frightening and mortifying at once. Thomas would never laugh at her...would he?

He reached out a hand to her, interrupting her thoughts. "You look cold, Maddie. Will you come sit by the fire with me?"

She rose from the sofa without hesitation, clasping his hand in hers as she seated herself on the floor beside him. The flames were still crackling merrily in the fireplace, throwing off heat that warmed her face and began to melt her fears.

"I am afraid that my path will never be secure unless I wed Kit," she said hesitantly, keeping Thomas's hand in hers and drawing strength from his touch. "I– I don't want to, and he doesn't want to be shackled to me. But there are times when I am sure that no one else will have me, that men use Kit as an excuse to ignore me."

She couldn't look up. If she saw derision in his eyes, or pity, or anything but complete acceptance she'd flee to her bedchamber and never come out.

His gentle voice broke through her dread. "No sane man would be looking for a reason to avoid you, Maddie. That I can swear to you."

"Do you think so?" She managed to lift her head and meet his gaze, but only just. She'd never been so candid with anyone except Kit, and the fear of rejection hung heavily around her heart.

"I know so," he said with conviction. "You're beautiful, you're intelligent, you're the kindest person I know..." He brushed the fingers of his free hand across her cheek. "Any man would be lucky to call you his wife."

Maddie's heart fluttered and she leaned into his touch, closing her eyes for a moment to fully take in the sensation. "You are very good at this comforting business," she replied with a little laugh.

"Is it working?"

"Maybe you should hold me again...just to make sure."

It was the boldest thing she'd ever said to a gentleman, but at that moment she didn't care. The only thing she wanted in the world was to be in Thomas's arms.

He obliged, wrapping his arms around her and tugging her closer. It wasn't enough, though. The way they were sitting made the embrace awkward and rather unsatisfying.

"This isn't working..." she muttered.

"I have a better idea." He stood and drew her to her feet, pulling her against his body and walking them toward the sofa. Before she could ask what he was doing, he dropped down onto the cushions and carried her down with him.

She let out a little yelp, then realized she'd settled in his lap. "Yes, this will do," she sighed, her arms encircling his broad shoulders as his came around her body.

He rested his cheek against hers, murmuring, "Good." Then his warm lips were at her ear. "Maddie, may I kiss you?"

Her heart was pounding and her skin radiated heat that had nothing to do with the fireplace. She'd never been kissed before, but she nodded her head faintly, gathering her courage. "I wish you would."

He brushed some loose hair from her face as she closed her eyes again, delighting in the tickling softness of his touch, the scent of leather-bound books that clung to his fingers. She sighed again and his mouth came down over hers, capturing her bottom lip in a caress unlike any she'd felt before.

All too soon he released her, but when he drew back she went forward. "Thomas," she breathed. "May I kiss *you*?"

"You may kiss me all night if you want to," he replied in a husky voice.

Feelings of triumph, of need, and of emotions she couldn't readily identify rushed through her. Whatever was happening, she wanted more.

Maddie leaned in. "An excellent idea."

Thomas was fairly floating when he rode out to the old house with Kit the next day. He hadn't spent the *whole* night kissing Maddie—they had somehow managed to part before midnight—but he'd finally had her alone, in his arms.

And she'd kissed him back. Thoroughly.

"I take it your evening went well," Kit grinned once they were a safe distance away from their hosts.

"Is it so obvious?"

Kit laughed. "Your feet have barely touched the floor since you woke this morning."

"Do you think mother noticed? Or Maddie's parents?" Thomas asked. They were supposed to think he was courting Maddie, of course, but he wasn't ready to declare his feelings to anyone else just yet. He'd only communicated them to Maddie herself in kisses instead of concrete promises, and barely a handful of hours earlier.

"Mother likely did, but she may not attribute your cheerfulness to Maddie specifically. Mrs. Hayward was too busy asking me if I would leave a room in the house untouched for my wife to decorate as she pleased."

Thomas couldn't help but roll his eyes, until they were stopped midway by a frightening thought. "You don't think they're fortune hunting, do you?" Kit's inheritance wasn't large, particularly when compared to more aristocratic estates, but it would provide him and his future family a comfortable existence. And that was more than Thomas could say about himself.

"If they were, they'd have tried to convince Maddie to throw me over and set her cap for Sir Anthony at the assembly." Kit paused, glancing over at Thomas. "She doesn't need permission to marry, brother. If someone were to ask for her hand, the decision would be hers alone."

"But would she go against her parents' wishes?"

"Have you asked her?"

Thomas hadn't asked Maddie anything last night other than, "Do you like that?" The subject of a possible future together simply hadn't come up. "No."

"Does she know how you feel about her?" Kit prompted.

She had to know he no longer considered her only a friend, but Thomas also hadn't mentioned the word *love* last night, nor any of its kin. "I don't know how to tell her."

That was partially true. Finding the right words to declare a love he'd felt for so long would be no easy task. But what if she was still intent on finding a suitor who wasn't a Mathison? What if she loved him in return, but was swept off her feet by another man while Thomas saved up his money?

"What if you just said, 'I care for you'?"

They turned in to the drive at the old house and trotted the horses to the newly repaired stable. Could it be that simple?

"What if she doesn't return my feelings?"

Kit jumped down from his horse. "What if she does?"

What if she does?

The thought rolled around in Thomas's head all morning as his hands performed whatever job Kit set them to. By the time they set out for the Hayward house that evening, Thomas had come up with a plan. Rather than walking through the front door and proclaiming his love for Maddie upon his return, he decided on a smaller first step. He would find a few moments alone with her and ask if she would be willing to make their courtship real, perhaps on a trial basis, for the remainder of his stay in Kent. If she said no, he would put the pieces of his heart back together and play her beau for a few more weeks, then retreat to Scotland and nurse his pain alone.

But if she said yes…

"You're smiling again, brother."

If she said yes, there would be more walks in the snow and kisses in the firelight. If she said yes, they would make new memories together.

"Don't forget we promised to pick up the post," Thomas called as Kit's horse danced away from his on the frozen road. Perhaps he could find a small gift for Maddie while they were in the village, as well. Some ribbon for her hair? The book of poetry she'd mentioned at the fête?

He shopped while Kit went to the post office, settling on a bottle of scent, smaller than he'd have liked it to be but from the heart all the same. He'd chosen one distilled from roses, and also had happily handed over the last of his coin for what had to be the only rose in bloom in England this time of year. The proprietor of the shop had a tiny hothouse in which she grew the flowers used to make the scent she sold, and she'd had a single blossom left. It was pink, not the red of her dress and his waistcoat, but Thomas didn't quibble over that small detail. When they came back in season—and he'd saved a bit of money again—he would buy her claret-colored roses every day if she wanted them.

Thomas and Kit returned to the Haywards' home, flushed with cold and in Thomas's case, anticipation.

"Ah, there you are," Mr. Hayward greeted them when they came through the front door. "We'd begun to wonder if you'd been waylaid at the old house."

Thomas felt Kit's elbow poke his ribs before he saw it, and forced a smile. No need to tip his hand before he spoke to Maddie herself. "We stayed in the village a bit longer than we'd planned, sir."

"But we did remember to pick up your post," Kit chimed in, ignoring the glare Thomas shot his way.

Kit handed over the bundle of letters

and began divesting himself of his outerwear, handing his greatcoat over to the maid-of-all-work to be dried before a fire. Thomas, conscious of the bottle and blossom tucked inside his pocket, elected to keep his coat, and carefully slung it over one arm as he made for the staircase and his bedchamber.

"Thomas, wait a moment," Mr. Hayward called after him. "There's a letter here for you."

Thomas retrieved it and brought it upstairs with him, tossing it onto his bed as he looked for a place to store his gifts. Perhaps their parents would attempt to leave Maddie alone with Kit again tonight, and he could give her the scent and rose then.

"Who's your letter from?" Kit asked, strolling into the room with a stack of his own letters.

"Oh, erm, I don't know." Thomas laid his coat onto the bed and took up the letter, breaking the seal with curiosity. "It's from our uncle." Unfolding the single page, he scanned the heavily slanted handwriting to see if it was something important.

"Thomas? What is it?" Kit asked a moment later. "You look as though the world is ending."

"I think mine is," he replied in a flat voice, unable to tear his eyes away from the horrible words. "Our uncle has closed his office and sailed for America."

"What?"

Thomas crumpled the letter and flung it against the nearest wall. "I no longer have employment."

Chapter 5

"THOMAS, WOULD YOU MIND TERRIBLY walking with me into the village?"

"Hmm?" He'd been sitting at the desk in his bedchamber, staring at his uncle's letter and hadn't heard Maddie enter the room.

"I know you just came from there," she continued, leaning against the open door, "but Cook needs some things for Christmas dinner and I wanted to do a little shopping anyway."

"Can't she get them herself?" he asked absently. Maddie's brows rose and her eyes widened in response. Thomas shook his head and he stood, closing the distance between them. "My apologies. Of course I'll accompany you if you'd like me to."

She searched his face for a moment before speaking again. "Is all well with you?"

Her voice was hesitant and he instinctively reached out to comfort her, sliding an arm around her waist and drawing her further into the room. "It is now," he smiled.

Maddie's arms came around his neck and she returned his smile, though not fully. "You could tell me if something were wrong."

If it was anything else, he might have told her then. It wasn't as though she was a stranger whose trust he was unsure of. But they'd only just begun this new version of their relationship—if that's even what it was—and he didn't want to burden her with his news until he'd had a chance to come to terms with it himself.

He opened his mouth to speak, then shut it again. What if sharing the burden made it easier to bear?

"You're absolutely right." It did—*might*—concern her, after all. If he couldn't make a living, he'd never be able to ask for her hand. "I received a letter from my uncle today."

"The one who employs you?"

He nodded, glad she was in his arms. He was the one being comforted now, but this was a tradition he was happy to continue.

If she didn't throw him over.

Thomas pushed the thought away. "Yes, the one who employs me. Or did. He's run off with an actress and closed his office."

She sucked in a quick breath. "And you have no employment now."

"No, I don't."

"Oh, Thomas..." She went up on her toes and tightened her hold on him. "I'm so sorry."

Her hair held the faint scent of gardenias and her body was warm against his. He closed his eyes and nuzzled her neck. *This.* This is the reaction he'd been hoping for. They had a long way to go if they were going to make a life together. Hell, he didn't even know if she thought of him as a genuine suitor. Was he still just Kit's little brother who she happened to like kissing?

"Maddie, this may not be the right time, but I need to know..." He loosened his hold on her and set her a little away from him. "Do you think you could ever care for me?"

"I have always cared for you," she smiled, palming his cheek.

He covered her hand with his own. "I don't mean as a friend, or as Kit's brother."

"You mean as a beau. A– a lover."

He nodded, kissing her palm and clasping her hand to his chest. "As a prospective husband."

She didn't respond, and the pounding of his heart filled the silence until he thought the wretched organ might explode. Was there so much to consider?

"You have always been my friend," she said at last. "But when you kissed me...nay, when I asked you for a faux courtship and you agreed without asking anything in return, I let myself consider the possibility."

"And what was the verdict?"

Pink crept up her neck and into her cheeks. "That if you wanted to change the plan, to make it a true courtship..." She paused, flattening her hand against his chest, where she could no doubt feel his poor heart beating to the rhythm of his anticipation. "I would be amenable to that."

His breathing hitched, then he sighed heavily in relief. It wasn't a declaration of love, but nearly so. And it had only been a few days since their night by the fire.

"Even though I have lost my employment? I have no money, Maddie, no home to offer you."

"Then don't offer yet," she said simply.

A surprised laugh burst from him. "Such an easy solution! Your parents won't mind?"

"My parents will mind terribly," she

replied all too matter-of-factly, patting his chest. "Not because of who you are, but because of your situation. We don't have to tell them, though. Not until we're ready to."

His relief mingled with a pinch of shame. When he was employed, Maddie was happy to have the world think he was courting her. But this temporary setback—and he sorely hoped it was only temporary—had her wanting to hide their relationship from her parents.

Her thumb traced the lapel of his cutaway coat. "What about your mother?"

He didn't relish the idea of explaining the situation when his mother still seemed to have her heart set on a match between Maddie and Kit, particularly when Kit had his inheritance and Thomas now had only the clothes on his back. "If we're not telling your parents, it's only fair not to tell my mother."

"Should we keep it from Kit?"

He couldn't quite read her expression

or body language. Was she uneasy about keeping so large a secret from her closest friend, or relishing the idea? "If I wasn't his brother, would you tell him about us?"

"I might," she answered, her brow furrowed in thought. "I likely would, actually. We tell each other nearly everything. If I wasn't his best friend, would *you* tell him about us?"

"Probably," Thomas admitted. "Kit and I have our shared confidences, too. But you *are* his best friend, and I am his brother. That might complicate matters."

Even as he spoke the words, Thomas didn't quite believe them. Kit had known for at least a year about Thomas's feelings for Maddie, and he'd never been anything but supportive.

"Let's not tell anyone at all," she suggested with a smile, tightening her arms around him and combing her fingers through his hair.

She wanted a clandestine courtship? It was almost too romantic a notion for his heart to bear, overwhelming the twinge of shame. "A secret for just the two of us."

"Does that mean I'll have to steal kisses from you on the way into the village?" She gave him what was probably supposed to be a sly look, but ended up giggling.

"You can't steal what's freely given." He released the hand he still held against his chest and wrapping her in his arms.

Leaning down to brush his lips over hers, he thrilled to his very fingertips when she responded in kind. He didn't know how, but by God he would find a way to make money again if it killed him. He would make himself worthy of her.

With thick mittens keeping Maddie's fingers warm, holding Thomas's hand on the way to the village was no easy task. Instead, she looped her arm through his, her body warming when he smiled down at her and dropped a kiss on the top of her bonnet.

The warmth lasted all the way to the first shop they visited, despite the snow that had begun to fall. They purchased the items Cook needed first, then continued on to the milliner's where Maddie spent a few minutes looking at ribbons in various colors. She wanted to spruce up her bonnet in time for church the next morning, but couldn't decide which color would be best.

"Green or blue?" she asked Thomas, removing her mittens and holding up each ribbon for his opinion.

He thought—or at least gave the appearance of thinking—about it for a moment, then pointed. "The blue one. It matches my eyes."

She couldn't keep the grin from her face, knowing full well that the other patrons of the shop would instantly peg her as a woman in love. But she didn't care what they thought, or who knew how she felt about Thomas.

Was it love? Maddie wasn't sure, but she

suspected it was. And while Thomas had made no declarations, he had been the one to propose a real courtship between them. Did that mean he cared for her, too, or that he thought he was rescuing her from a life of lonely spinsterhood?

He brushed his hand across her back. "Anything else you need here?"

She turned a little and tilted her face up to meet his gaze, pleased to find a version of her own foolish grin smiling down at her. "No, just this."

She purchased her blue ribbon and they walked across the street to the tiny bookshop where she hoped to find a new novel to add to her collection.

"Mama is not so keen on my reading habits," Maddie remarked, running a finger across the spines of *The Vindictive Spirit, A Novel In Four Volumes.*

"Your mother doesn't like you to read?" Thomas's brows drew down in confusion.

Maddie shook her head. "It's not reading itself she objects to, it's my taste in reading material." She tapped the cover of volume four. "For example, if I brought this home she'd lecture me about the impropriety of reading such things and force me to return it."

"What are you allowed to read?"

"Mostly improving tracts for girls and women," Maddie replied with a frown. "They aren't very entertaining."

He chuckled. "I wouldn't think so. What is it you're after today?"

Maddie tapped the novel's cover again and took a step closer to him. "I already have volumes one and two, and I've been aching to know what happens next."

"Maddie Hayward, rebellious daughter," he quipped quietly. "Your secret is safe with me."

"That makes two, then," she said, sending him a furtive little smile. What other secrets would they share before New Year's Day?

She scooped up volume three of *The Vindictive Spirit* and made her way to the counter, surreptitiously scanning the other shelves for something Thomas might like. She was already halfway done with the scarf she was knitting him for Christmas, but she might be able to save enough of her pin money to purchase a book for his birthday in two months' time.

They made one more stop at the tea shop for the special biscuits Cook wanted to serve after Christmas dinner, then headed back. When they came within sight of the Haywards' house, Thomas stopped her with a hand on her arm.

"Where is your novel?"

Her eyes widened. In the blissful haze that had developed during their walk home, she'd forgotten all about the forbidden book. "It's here," she said, pulling it from the bag Thomas carried containing their items.

He unbuttoned his greatcoat and slipped the book inside. "If anyone asks, I'll tell them it's mine."

"You know what our parents will think

of you if you tell them you've been reading a Minerva Press novel."

They'd think something was wrong with his mind, but Thomas only shrugged. "They may think what they like."

Maddie shot a quick glance at the house —still too far away for anyone to recognize them—and drew him down to her for a kiss. "Thomas Mathison, you are the noblest of gentlemen."

"Anything for you," he said softly.

For the rest of the afternoon and into the evening there was always someone with Maddie, making it impossible for her to retrieve her book from Thomas. But when Thomas excused himself from the evening entertainment to go write letters, their predictable parents once again made an effort to retire before Kit did, leaving Maddie alone with him in the parlor not too long after dinner.

"A last attempt to wring a Christmas proposal of marriage from you, no doubt," Maddie teased him, noting that their machinations no longer bothered her the way they had.

"Not from me, at least," Kit returned with a wink, prying himself from his chair. "Thomas asked me to pass along a message to you—he asks that you stay here and wait for him, and that he'll return your book tonight."

"Excellent."

Kit's eyes lingered on her for a long moment, but he didn't ask the questions that were probably running through his mind. Instead he simply smiled and took himself off to bed.

Only a few minutes later, Thomas appeared in the doorway carrying his greatcoat over one arm with the other hidden behind his back. "Would you like some company?"

"Yes," she said, meeting him halfway across the room for an embrace. "Oh! You're cold!"

He draped the coat over a chair and dropped a kiss on her hair, laying one freezing hand across the bare skin of her neck. "Ah, but you're so warm."

She gave a little shriek and pulled away laughing. "I didn't realize writing letters required you to go outside."

"I saw something on our way home from the village this afternoon that I wanted to go back for." He pulled his other hand out from behind his back. "Perhaps you'll help me thaw out by the fire?"

Maddie poked at the mass of leaves and stems Thomas was holding. "What is it?"

"Mistletoe," he said with a small smile. "I didn't have time to make it into a proper kissing bough, but I think this will do."

"Yes," she breathed, wrapping her arms around him. "I believe it will."

His lips were warm and soft when they met hers, and she couldn't help but sigh. "This—you—are more than I ever hoped for, Thomas."

He kissed her once more, slowly, skillfully, until her toes began to curl in her shoes. "I have one more thing for you, darling," he said murmured she'd opened her eyes again.

He left her for a moment and fished around inside his coat, coming up with the novel she'd purchased that afternoon. "I thought perhaps we could read it together. You'll have to tell me what happened in the first two volumes, of course."

"What a wonderful idea."

They settled together on the floor before the fire, Thomas leaning back against the sofa and wrapping an arm around Maddie as she curled up beside him, resting her head on his chest. She dutifully recounted the events of the novel up through the end of volume two, then relaxed against his body when he began to read aloud.

His voice washed over her in warm waves and she let her eyes close. She hadn't realized it until very recently, but if she'd been told she could have anything her heart desired for Christmas, this was what she would have chosen.

The clock struck midnight as he came to the end of a chapter and Maddie savored the contentment washing over her.

"Merry Christmas, my love," she murmured.

She felt his breath catch, his heart pounding in his chest before he answered.

"Merry Christmas, sweetheart."

Chapter 6

Thomas slept little after seeing Maddie to her bedchamber just before one o'clock in the morning. He'd lain in bed staring up at the ceiling, listening to Kit's breathing fill the silence as he relived every moment of the evening with Maddie. She'd been warm and soft in his arms, calling him "my love" and looking at him like he was the only man in the world for her. Thomas tried to remember the last time he'd been this euphoric, but nothing he'd previously experienced even came close.

By the time the sun began to peek over the horizon, Thomas had decided to ask for

Maddie's hand in marriage. Not right away, no matter how badly he wanted to. With a decision this important, it was prudent to wait and make sure what he thought he wanted was truly what he wanted. And Maddie deserved that same opportunity. He had no schedule to keep, but perhaps he could find some time alone with her on Twelfth Night. They could take a walk together back to that copse of trees where he first held her, and he could ask her there.

He finally drifted off to sleep with a smile on his face and the scent of her perfume still clinging to his shirt.

The next thing he knew, Kit was shaking him awake with instructions to wash and dress for church.

"Already?" he croaked.

"Late night?" Kit grinned.

Thomas pulled himself to a sitting position and rubbed his eyes. "Yes."

"Was it worth it?"

Thomas felt his mouth pull into what

was probably a foolish smile and nodded. "Yes."

"Good," Kit replied. "I'll remind you of that when you begin nodding off at dinner."

Thomas managed to stay awake during the service despite the vicar's determination to put everyone to sleep. He also made it through the afternoon meal, trading sly glances with his beloved across the table. But once the meal was finished, he retired to his bedchamber hoping to snatch a couple of hours' sleep before the evening's celebrations began.

Once again, Thomas had a difficult time falling asleep. But this time it wasn't euphoria that kept him awake—it was fear.

What happened if Maddie said yes to his proposal? After the excitement died down and they began making arrangements for the wedding, for their life together...what then? The reason he had no schedule to keep was because he no longer had a way to make a living. He had a little money put by, certainly, but not enough to support two people. Maddie would have a dowry, too, but he doubted it was a large one. Would it be enough for them to live on?

Probably not.

He rose from the bed and stumbled over to the little writing desk in the corner of the room. He couldn't ask Maddie to marry him until he could support her, and he couldn't support her until he found work again. The only logical thing to do, then, was to begin writing letters. Someone he knew, or who had known his uncle, might be in need of a clerk and the only way to find out was to ask.

He was still hunched over the desk when Kit came to fetch him for dinner some hours later.

"I thought you wanted to sleep," his brother said, swinging the chamber door open wide.

"I did," Thomas replied, not looking up from his work, "but I couldn't."

"Well, everyone is gathering in the

parlor. You still have a few minutes to dress for dinner, but I'd hurry if I were you." Kit gave him a playful slap on the back. "If I can distract mother long enough, you'll be able to sit beside Maddie tonight."

Thomas lifted his head, meeting his brother's eyes but not really seeing them. "Yes, that sounds good."

He returned to the letter he was composing, determined to finish it before he did anything else. He could walk into the village first thing tomorrow to post it and the others he'd completed.

"I'll see you downstairs, then, I suppose," Kit muttered, shrugging his shoulders as he exited the room.

"I'll be down shortly," Thomas called belatedly after his brother.

He managed to find a clean shirt and his best tailcoat, washing hurriedly in the basin before changing his clothing and dashing down the staircase. The assemblage was just about to go in to dinner when he arrived in the parlor, and Kit had their mother on his arm.

"Excellent," Thomas said under his breath, approaching Maddie. "May I?" he asked her, offering his arm.

Her grin was as large and foolish as his had been the night before. "Yes," she said softly, twining her arm with his.

She was wearing a green gown tonight, but he could smell delicate roses about her instead of her usual perfume, reminding him of the little bottle and accompanying flower he'd hidden away in his bedchamber. If they could find some time alone together tonight, he could give them to her. Even better if he could locate that bit of mistletoe he'd scavenged the day before.

But first, he had more letters to write. He already had letters for his uncle's friends in Edinburgh, but there were other people who might be able to help. Thomas's father had lived in London for some years before marrying—perhaps his mother would remember something of her late husband's friends and business associates.

"Did you hear me?"

"Hmm?"

He glanced in the direction the voice had come from and found Maddie staring at him, her brows lifted in inquiry. "Oh, my apologies. I missed the last thing you said."

"I think you missed everything I said," she replied, placing a slice of roast goose on her plate. "Where is your head today, Thomas?"

"Stuck on practical matters, I'm afraid," he said, poking a bit of carrot with his fork.

"Anything I should know about?"

He shook his head, not wanting to have this particular conversation surrounded by their families. "Not at the moment."

Her eyes flicked back to his and held his gaze, then returned to her food. "Later, then."

He speared the carrot and popped it into his mouth. "Perhaps."

What had happened to her affectionate, attentive Thomas? When Kit said his brother hadn't slept well the night before, Maddie brushed off Thomas's aloofness as fatigue. But dinner progressed and the families moved into the parlor for whatever evening entertainment her mother had cooked up, and Thomas still seemed far away.

Well, there was no rule that said he had to hang on her every word, was there? Neither would she want him to. But such an abrupt change from his demeanor the previous evening made Maddie wonder if something bigger was afoot.

She waited for a break in the revels—singing carols and sharing stories of Christmases past—to try to draw him away from the group for a quick word.

"Thomas, could you help me with something?" she asked, tapping a finger on his shoulder to gain his attention.

"Perhaps Kit should help you," her mother responded from her place on the sofa.

"No, Mama, I need Thomas for this."

His eyes swung to hers and he flashed her a smile—a genuine, warm smile of the kind she'd come to expect from him. "I am at your service."

"Thank you," she said, returning the smile. "It's this way."

Maddie gestured toward the door and Thomas followed her into the hallway, giving her an odd look when she continued on toward the dining room.

"What exactly do you need my help with?" he asked, trailing behind her.

"Nothing," she replied sheepishly, pushing open the dining room door and tugging him inside. "I merely wanted a moment alone with you."

She reached for his hand and he allowed her to take it, but his posture was rigid, the expression on his face somewhere between discomfort and fear.

"Thomas, what's wrong?"

He shook his head. "Nothing you need

concern yourself about."

Maddie held his hand in both of hers, taking a step closer to him as she studied his features. "If something has upset you, then it concerns me. I'd like to help if I can."

"Nothing has upset me," he snapped back.

She flinched, releasing his hand. "Yes, I can see that."

"I'm sorry, darling," he said softly, reaching for her hand and clasping it once more. "I'm just having a difficult time dealing with my sudden lack of employment."

Well that certainly made sense. What would she do if someone sent her a letter saying she no longer had access to a home or the basic necessities of life? She certainly wouldn't be cheerful about it.

"I have some news that may help," she said, a hopeful note in her voice. "There was a letter from my grandmother in the post you brought home. Her current companion is to be married, and she wants me to come live with her in the companion's place."

"How is that helpful?" Thomas seemed genuinely curious, though there was a hard edge to the question.

Maddie took a breath and held it for an extra fraction of a second. "In addition to the pin money I have from Papa, I'd have a small wage from Gran, too. She only lives a few miles away, so if you stayed with Kit you could..." She let her voice trail off and tried to scrutinize his expression again. "Are you listening to me, Thomas?"

"Yes," he replied with a weary air. "You're saying that because I can't provide for you, you're going to work for a living yourself."

"What?" For the second time, Maddie broke physical contact with him. "No—this is as much for Gran as it is for anything else. She needs someone to look after her, and she doesn't want to leave the house my grandfather built for her." She squinted slightly, confused by his lack of empathy. "I thought you'd understand that. The money is just an added benefit."

"What am I to do in the meantime?" he asked, pulling out a chair from the dining table and dropping onto it. "Am I to wait until you've saved enough money? Then you'll propose marriage to me?"

She took a step back, her voice quiet when she answered. "You could live with Kit, and give lessons in Latin and Greek until you find something more to your liking."

His only response was to sigh and look past her, and Maddie could feel her hands clenching into fists. "What difference does it make where the money comes from, Thomas? The sooner we save enough, the sooner we can be together."

"Will you still want to be with me when I'm a bitter man who can't provide for his own wife? Because that is likely what I'll become without a real place in the world."

She took another breath, a deep one

this time, and let it out slowly. "If I'm earning money, you'll have time to find yourself a new situation. Can't you see that? Then you'll be able to find employment that fulfills you, my Gran will be cared for, and we won't have to wait so long to be wed. That is, if you actually want to marry me."

"Perhaps you'd be better off with another man," he replied in a voice devoid of emotion. "Wasn't that your plan all along?"

Maddie felt as if she'd been struck. She instinctively covered her heart with her hand as if to protect a wound there. "My plan was to find someone who wasn't Kit; someone who would love me and who I could love in return, who would be my partner in life," she choked out. "I thought I had succeeded."

"You have succeeded in finding a man with no livelihood, Maddie," he returned quietly. "I saw you in the village, flitting from shop to shop. You were enjoying yourself immensely. How much will you enjoy wearing the same two dresses all the time because we can't afford new clothing? Or having no books to read because we've sold them all to pay for food?"

"Thomas—"

"I don't think you've thought this through," he continued, rising from the chair. "It doesn't matter how much we might love each other if we don't have enough money to live on. And I don't need to be reminded of how little I have to offer you every day of our lives. Perhaps you should marry my brother after all—he, at least, would be able to take proper care of you."

He strode from the room, shutting the door carefully behind him, leaving Maddie alone with the furniture.

"I think that was the end of our courtship," she told the table, running a finger over its smooth, cold surface. "Thomas, like all the others, thinks I belong with Kit."

Chapter 7

Instead of returning to the parlor and rejoining the two families, Thomas continued on to the staircase and made for the bedchamber he shared with his brother. He wasn't sure what he was going to do there, only that the very last thing he wanted was to sing songs and celebrate.

He entered the room and sat down on his bed, bracing his hands against the mattress. What had just happened? What had he done?

He'd put his own feelings aside for Maddie's future happiness—that's what he had done. The Haywards weren't wealthy, but the status Maddie would sink to as Thomas's wife was more than he could bear. She deserved better than he could give her. She deserved better than *him*.

A knock sounded on the door a split second before the door swung open. "Are you well, brother?"

"Go away, Kit."

"I'll take that as a no." Kit entered the room and closed the door behind him. "What happened? I found Maddie crying in the dining room."

Thomas tried to ignore the stabbing pain in his chest and concentrate on getting Kit out of there. He knew that if he didn't give his brother at least some information, Kit would remain in the room until he wrung out every detail. "I set Maddie free."

"You what?"

"I told her she was better off with a man who had more money than I do."

Kit stood in the center of the room, staring at Thomas. "Why would you do such a foolish thing? I thought you loved her."

"I did it *because* I love her," Thomas replied, unwilling to lift his gaze from the carpet. "Perhaps I'll find employment again and save enough money to support a wife, but she shouldn't have to sit by and wait to see if that happens."

"Did you ask her what *she* wanted?"

Thomas's gaze dropped lower, to a stocking peeking out from underneath his bed. "She wants to become a paid companion for her grandmother, to make money when I can't."

Kit grunted at that. "And that hurt your pride."

His tone was gentler, more understanding, and Thomas ventured a glance at his brother. "Quite possibly. But that's not what this is about."

"No. It's about your insecurities, isn't it?" Kit crossed his arms over his chest and frowned down at Thomas. "Things were actually going well with Maddie. I may have been keeping my distance, but I saw the two of you together enough to know your feelings for her were growing...and mutual. Then you stumble over one stupid rock in your path and you quit the race altogether."

Thomas took a deep breath and let it out slowly as he stood, starting a list in his mind of the things he would need to take with him. If he couldn't get rid of Kit, then he would remove himself from the house. "There was no race, Kit."

"I know that—it's a metaphor. A poor one, perhaps, but never mind. The point is that at the first sign of trouble, you gave up."

Thomas found his hat and winter gloves, tossing them on the bed, and attempted to don his greatcoat. The deuced thing was acting as if it had a mind of its own. "I didn't *want* to let her go, Kit."

"I believe you." Kit stepped aside as Thomas flung his arm out in an effort to tame his coat. "But it was easier to do that than to face your problems, wasn't it? How afraid are you to allow someone to depend on you?"

Thomas looked at his brother, then yanked on the lapels of the greatcoat. "I can't have Maddie without money."

"You can't have Maddie if you're unwilling to work through your troubles, either."

Thomas rolled his eyes, but didn't respond. The famous Mathison stubborn streak was rising up again—likely in both of them—and he was not in the mood to waste his time.

Kit went on with his lecture as if Thomas was a dolt completely incapable of intelligent thought. "She presented you with a perfectly good way for the two of you to be together, and you pretended as though it was beneath you. Do you know how much that hurt her?"

Thomas felt the pain in his chest again —the last thing he'd ever want to do was hurt Maddie. He shoved the thought away, though, and continued dressing to go outdoors. What he needed right now was to get away from here, away from the judgment of his brother and the wreck of his dreams. If Maddie truly wanted him, she wouldn't have been so quick to throw his inadequacies in his face.

Perhaps she didn't want him that badly after all.

He picked up his heavy winter gloves from the bed and pulled them on. "Does she know how much she's hurt me?"

Thomas snatched up his hat from his bed and marched out the door. He heaved a sigh of relief when he made it to the front door of the house without seeing anyone else about—the only thing he wanted right then was to be alone.

He walked the two miles to his childhood home at full speed, hoping to burn off some of the anger and pain that boiled inside him. But they only seemed to build. Perhaps he should have expected Maddie to act the way she did—he was, after all, a second son with nothing but his mother's love, and one couldn't pay the rent with that.

But Thomas had expected his brother to take his side, and Kit had sided with her. That hurt more than Thomas was willing to admit.

"I really shouldn't be surprised, though," he said to the front door of the old house as he put the key in the lock and turned it. "If he hadn't been so partial to her, none of this would have happened in the first place."

Thomas burst into the house and shut the door firmly behind him, blocking out that thought as well. He was in an untenable situation. He wished he'd never kissed Maddie, never caressed her, never opened his heart to her. He couldn't quite bring himself to wish he'd never met her, but how much less painful would the loss of his employment—and his ability to make his own way in life—be if he'd never come to Kent this Christmas?

Would his uncle's departure have hurt if Thomas had stayed in Edinburgh? Absolutely.

"But I didn't stay," he said through gritted teeth. "I came here and found love. This was my chance to have everything I wanted, and it's gone."

He stomped around the house collecting firewood, kindling, and a tinderbox, shucking his outer garments as he went, the vigorous movement warming him even in the chilly house. Once he got the fire going, Thomas found himself unable to sit still. Well, Kit had showed him how to make some of the small repairs—perhaps that would be a good way to spend the rest of the evening.

Then at least something good would come of the day.

Maddie ran into her chamber and threw herself down on her bed, frustration boiling over into anger. Why wouldn't Thomas just listen to her? Maybe working as her grandmother's companion wasn't going to bring in a lot of money, but it would certainly help. And he'd dismissed the idea as if she'd insulted him by even suggesting it. Was this just a one-time occurrence? Or was this how he would always treat her when there was a problem?

If this was how he dealt with setbacks, then perhaps it was better that they parted.

A knock sounded on her door, and she slid off the bed to answer it. When she saw her best friend waiting with open arms, her throat became tight again.

"I know I'm supposed to keep my distance," he said, his voice low and serious, "but I thought you might need a friendly ear and a good hug tonight."

"I heard footsteps and the front door, and assumed that was Thomas leaving. You didn't go with him?"

Kit dropped his empty arms and shook his head. "He's my brother and I love him, but in this case he's being an ass. I don't know what got into him."

Maddie opened the door wider and gestured Kit inside. "He's more interested in money than he is in me."

"I doubt that very much," Kit replied, closing the door behind him. "I probably shouldn't be telling his secrets, but in this case I think it's justified. He's loved you for some time now, and he was over the moon when you two decided to pursue a romantic relationship."

Her heart did a little flip—Thomas loved her!—until she recalled the way he'd reacted to Gran's offer. "He's not acting like it."

"I know." Kit held out his arms again. "And I'm sorry for it."

Maddie finally allowed herself to embrace her friend, letting the comfort and relief of his arms push the turmoil from her mind. "You aren't the one who should be sorry, Kit, but I appreciate the thought."

He gave her a squeeze and pulled back a little to look her in the eyes. "Is there anything I can do?"

"You're doing it," she said, giving him a weak smile.

"All right, then." He pulled her close again and rested his cheek against her temple. "I'll just stay right here until you tell me to go."

"Good." And it was good. She'd missed Kit so much these past weeks, but she missed Thomas now, too. If he hadn't been such an ass, as Kit had called him, he would be the one holding her tonight. "Do you think he'll come around, Kit?"

"I certainly hope so. No one could love you mo—"

She drew back and tried to read the expression on his face, but he wasn't looking at her. "What?" Maddie followed his gaze and discovered her parents standing just inside the open door, her mother's hand still on the knob.

"Is it official now?" her mother asked, clasping her hands to her chest. "Have you said yes?"

Maddie knew she should have leaped away from Kit, should have tried to explain the situation. But if months and months of protest hadn't convinced her parents that she wasn't going to marry Kit, a last minute denial wouldn't either. She suddenly felt weary of the whole thing and bowed her head against Kit's chest, closing her eyes.

Her mother, predictably, exclaimed her happiness and ran off to find Mrs. Mathison. Maddie heard her father say something to Kit about settlements in a gruff voice, then he, too, was gone.

"You didn't contradict them," Kit said softly when they were alone again. "Do you want to wed me, Maddie?"

"Would it really be so bad?" Her voice was low, small, as if she didn't want anyone to truly hear what she was saying. "Everyone would finally stop nagging us about it."

He gripped her chin firmly and tilted her head up to meet his blue eyes, so like his brother's. "That is a poor reason to choose a spouse, Maddie Hayward, and you know it."

He was right, of course, but she tried again anyway. "Would it be so awful to have me as your wife? Nothing about our relationship would have to change," she added quickly. "We could carry on as we always have, just living in the same house together."

Kit released her chin, then released her body from his embrace. "We could. If that was what you truly wanted. It would mean you'd never have the chance to work things out with Thomas. And there would be no children."

Maddie's mind wandered back to her conversation with Thomas by the bonfire at the Midwinter Fête and the image of his curly-haired family. She'd unconsciously placed herself in that picture over the past few days, smiling brightly back at Thomas as he taught the children to fish. But that's all it would be if she and Kit were wed—an image in her mind. Kit would most certainly make a good father, but they would have to share a bed to produce children. Yet the thought of even kissing Kit made her mildly nauseated. She loved him, certainly, but as her friend not her lover.

He must have sensed her hesitation, because he set his hands on her shoulders and bent his head to catch her eye. "Would you like some time to think about it?"

"No," she answered immediately. She was sick unto death of thinking about marriage with Kit. Then, "Wait, yes. I would like some time to think about it, and I suspect you would, too. If we're going to do this, we'd better both be sure about it."

"Indeed." He smiled and gave her shoulders a squeeze. "I'll leave you to your thoughts for the night, then. But if you should need anything, I am just a couple of doors away."

"Thank you."

Maddie watched as he let himself out then flopped back onto her bed, staring up at the ceiling with unseeing eyes. She didn't know if Thomas would ever speak to her again, nor was she sure she wanted him to at the moment, even though he'd all but professed his love for her and she for him. Instead, she was actually considering giving in to the pressure society and their families had been putting on her for months—perhaps years—and marrying Kit.

How had things progressed to this point?

Wedding Kit would be the easy way out, of course. She would have a home, a companion she cared for, the independence she longed for, and the ease of never having to worry about money. But if that was all she wanted out of life, she could live out her days with Gran and never think of marriage again.

Did she want more? Did she *deserve* more?

Did Kit?

If she married Kit, she wouldn't just be sacrificing her own chance at love but his, too.

She rolled onto her stomach and buried her face in the red counterpane. Life had been so much easier when the worst thing she could think of was catching a bigger fish than her best friend.

Chapter 8

THOMAS AWOKE IN HIS OLD bedchamber, his long legs hanging off the side of the bed. Pushing an aging quilt from his body and pulling himself into a sitting position, he realized he'd fallen asleep laying in the wrong direction.

And fully clothed.

He tried to run a hand through his hair, but met resistance from what was certainly a tangled mess of curls. He'd slept restlessly, plagued with odd, disjointed dreams that disturbed him even though he couldn't remember anything specific about them.

Then the memory of the previous day's falling out with Maddie flooded back into his mind and he sighed, dropping his head into his hands. She'd been upset, of course. But what he could no longer ignore was the shock written on her features when he'd said his state of mind was none of her concern, the pain he knew he had caused when he told her she was better off with Kit because he had money.

"Kit was right," he mumbled. "I am an ass."

The cold of the room crept under the layers of his clothing, and Thomas realized the fire he'd lit the night before had gone out. Wrapping himself in the quilt, he chastised himself for forgetting to bank the fire before he'd gone to bed. Then he chastised himself some more for the way he'd treated Maddie. He'd been so caught up in his perceived inadequacies that he'd rejected Maddie's attempt to help. For that was what she'd been doing when she told him about her grandmother's suggested arrangement. But he'd been too self-centered to see it.

"Have I ruined our future before it could even begin?"

Perhaps not. One of the things he loved about Maddie was her compassionate nature. Oh, she had been the first person to tell him or Kit when they'd done something stupid as adolescents, but she'd also been quick to forgive when presented with genuine remorse and the desire to make the situation right again.

"And I most certainly want to make this situation right again." He clambered off the bed and dropped the quilt onto the floor. "Will she see me if I return to the Haywards' house?"

There was only one way to find out. As he set about tidying his appearance, he tried to plan out what to say to her. "I'm sorry I hurt you," definitely needed to be said, but what else? How to explain the temporary madness that had come over him? Could he assure her it would never happen again?

Another thought halted him in his tracks. What if she wasn't alone?

If Kit was with her—and he probably was—he could be convinced to leave them. But if she was with her parents and his mother, Thomas wasn't sure he'd be able to get her alone.

Dear God, he might have to beg for Maddie's forgiveness while both their families looked on.

A shiver passed through his body. "It should be a private moment," he said to a portrait of his great-grandfather, who probably would have agreed with Thomas's assessment. "But if I have to humble myself in front of the entire county to return to her good graces, then that is what I will do."

When he was satisfied with his appearance, he went hunting for the rose and bottle of scent he'd procured from the shop in the village. He remembered unexpectedly finding both in the pockets of his tailcoat shortly after he'd arrived at the old house, remembered taking them out and putting them somewhere he couldn't see them, where he wouldn't be reminded of who they'd been meant for.

Ah-ha! He discovered both items on top of a tall bookshelf in what had been his father's study. The rose was wilted and rather worse for the wear, but the bottle of scent was intact. That would have to do, unless he found something else on the way to the Haywards' home—unlikely in this weather.

No matter, the scent would do nicely. He'd originally meant it as a gift simply because he'd wanted to give Maddie something, but it would serve just as well as an I'm-sorry offering and a belated Christmas gift.

Thomas located his greatcoat and hat—thrown haphazardly over the banister when he'd entered the house—and headed out into the freezing cold.

"Are you sure you want to do this?" Kit looked down at Maddie, his blond brows raised as he asked the question.

He was giving her the chance to back out. No one else knew about their decision except the two of them, and they didn't have to announce it to their families *now*. But Maddie knew their parents would have to be told at some point. Now was as good a time as any.

"Yes," she said resolutely. It hadn't taken her long to figure out what—or who —she really wanted after Kit had left her to her own devices the night before, and what would be best for all involved. She'd known it since she'd sat down to breakfast with the Mathison brothers the first morning of their visit, and Kit had agreed when she went to him first thing that morning with her answer.

"All right then."

Their parents were gathered in the

Haywards' parlor wishing the blustery weather to perdition when Maddie entered the room at Kit's side. All three heads swiveled in their direction and the conversation had died by the time Maddie came to a halt in front of the fireplace, with Kit taking his place to the left and just behind her.

"Mama, Papa, Mrs. Mathison..." Maddie began with confidence, but with three sets of eyes upon her—the eyes of the people who had dismissed her wishes for months and months in favor of their own—her resolve began to melt. She felt Kit's warm hand on her back and took a calming breath, then started again. "Kit and I have an announcement to make—"

"Wait!"

Maddie turned toward the door as Thomas rushed in, still wearing his greatcoat and hat and dusted with snow. "Thomas, what are you—"

"Please don't marry Kit," he interrupted, tossing his hat onto the nearest chair and running a hand through his disheveled auburn curls.

Maddie heard Kit's low chuckle behind her and she managed a smile, despite the thudding of her heart. "I wasn't going to."

"You weren't?" Thomas asked, stopping short.

"You weren't?" Maddie's mother echoed from the sofa. "What announcement were you and Kit going to make?"

"We were going to announce that we'd decided never to marry each other," Kit supplied helpfully. "Maddie and I hoped that you all would honor our wishes if we told everyone together."

Thomas's hands were cold and bare when they enveloped hers, but he was smiling broadly and her body warmed at his touch. "Good. Then I still have a chance to apologize to you."

"As you should," Kit returned with a pointed look at his brother.

"Perhaps we should speak privately,"

Maddie offered, squeezing Thomas's hands. If there was an apology awaiting her, would there also be an opportunity to have a real conversation about their future?

His smile took on a relieved quality, and his whole body seemed to relax. "Yes. That's a good idea."

With a quick glance at their families, she led him from the parlor around to the dining room, where he'd told her to find a man with money only the day before. Once he'd closed the door behind them, he clasped her free hand once more and rubbed his thumbs over both her hands.

"I'm sorry, Maddie," he said without preamble. "I got so wrapped up in trying to meet some arbitrary definition of worthiness—and failing—that I completely missed the point of courtship."

He stepped closer and the scent of pine and wool emanated from the greatcoat he still wore.

"And what's that?" she asked softly, her blood pounding in her ears.

"To be together," he replied, resting his forehead against hers. "Will you forgive my utter foolishness, darling? Might we resume our courtship?"

She wanted with all her being to say yes, but there were things they needed to discuss first. She pulled back slightly to look into his blue eyes. "I do forgive you, Thomas. But what happens the next time we must deal with a problem? Will you insist on making all the decisions without even talking to me? What about when you and I have a disagreement? Are you going to shut me out until you miss me enough to apologize?"

Thomas drew back as if he'd been stung, then bowed his head. "You're insinuating that I've been a boor as well as a numbskull, and I deserve that. I have been."

"And I deserve answers to my questions," Maddie replied quietly.

He blinked, then lifted his gaze to hers. "You are an intelligent woman, Maddie Hayward, and I was an idiot to dismiss that fact. If I'd have kept my head in the first place, we could have had a real conversation about our future and avoided all this turmoil. I promise you I won't forget that."

"We can still have that conversation," she said, her lips curving into a slow smile. "If you're willing."

"I am, and we should," he replied with an answering smile. "Might we delay it just a few moments longer, though? There's one more thing I would like to do."

He released her and reached into his pockets, producing a small glass bottle in one hand and a familiar clump of leaves in the other.

"What on earth?"

"Belated Christmas gifts," he said, extending the hand with the bottle.

She plucked it from his palm and opened it, closing her eyes in pleasure as the scent of roses filled the air. "My favorite," she sighed.

"Is that why you wore it the night of the

assembly?"

Maddie's eyes popped open. "You noticed?"

"You usually wear gardenias." He licked his lips and shifting his weight from one foot to the other. "But the scent of roses will always remind me of you now."

She set the bottle down on the dining room table and slid her arms around Thomas's middle. "That makes it the perfect gift."

He wrapped one arm around her and pressed his cheek to hers. "The second one is for both of us."

"Is that what I think it is?" she murmured, warm and content against him.

He nodded, the stubble on his unshaven face bristling against her skin. "Mistletoe."

She drew back to examine the green mass he held in his other hand, then burst out laughing. "So it is."

"May I kiss you under it?"

"I think that's an excellent idea."

He obliged her, brushing his lips over

hers before tossing the mistletoe onto the table and pulling her body against his with both arms. "I love you, Maddie. I can't promise you I'll never let my insecurities get the better of me again, but I'll do everything I can to keep them in check."

"Including coming to me for help?" she asked, tilting her head slightly to one side.

"That," he said, leaning his forehead against hers, "will be my first step. And I hope it would be yours, too, in a similar situation."

"Good." She sighed softly and stroked a hand down his back. "And yes, I would come to you for help if I needed it. I love you, and your support—your emotional support—is important to me."

"Good."

"Like now," she continued with a sly smile. "I think I might need to be kissed again. Can you help me with that?"

He dipped his head, pausing just before capturing her lips once more. "With pleasure."

Epilogue

━━━◦◦◦◦◦━━━

Kent, England
Spring, 1814

"THEY'LL BE HERE ANY MOMENT, Gran," Maddie called from the kitchen in the little house her grandfather had built so long ago. "Will you keep them entertained while I finish up in here?"

"Don't you worry," Gran called back. "Your young men are in good hands."

Maddie exchanged glances with the maid-of-all-work who was chopping vegetables beside her, and they both giggled. Gran would no doubt be talking their ears off before the food had even half finished cooking. And both Mathison men would enjoy themselves immensely.

Kit had offered his brother a home until he could find work or save enough money to open his own office and Thomas had accepted, giving some of the local boys lessons in Latin and Greek to earn his keep. Once Maddie had settled into her grandmother's household, Gran had begun inviting the brothers to dine with them every week and would choose a story from the newspaper to discuss with them.

Maddie wiped her hands on a towel as she walked into the parlor. "What are you going to talk about tonight?"

"Some company is installing gas lighting in Westminster," Gran replied, reaching for the newspaper and seeking out the story she'd marked. "Ah yes, the Gas Light and Coke Company. Gas lighting—can you imagine?"

For a moment, Maddie did imagine it. She'd never been anywhere outside Kent, but she'd seen sketches of the Houses of Parliament and Westminster Bridge, and she pictured herself standing with Thomas under the new gaslights. If they actually were to visit Westminster there would be other people going about their business, of course, but in Maddie's mind the two of them stood alone on the bridge in each other's arms.

"I think it would be beautiful," she smiled, leaning against the door frame.

A knock on the door interrupted her musings, but her smile returned when she answered it and found Thomas and Kit on the doorstep. "You're just in time," Maddie grinned. "Gran's got a good one for you today."

Kit greeted her and gave her shoulder a little squeeze, then moved off toward the parlor to say hello to Gran, giving Maddie and Thomas a few precious moments alone together.

He pulled a small tangled ball of leaves from his pocket and held it over her head.

"I believe you're standing underneath some mistletoe, Miss Hayward."

She laughed, pushing his hand away and wrapping her arms around him. "If you keep bringing that stuff every week, there won't be any left for Christmas," she laughed.

"Maybe I'll learn to cultivate it," he returned with a wink.

"You don't need it." She went up on her tiptoes and murmured in his ear, "If you want to kiss me all you have to do is ask."

"May I kiss you, Maddie, my love?" he whispered softly.

"Yes," she breathed.

They had only enough time for a brief brushing of lips before Gran's voice called out, "Did you two get lost on the way to the parlor?"

Thomas chuckled, running a finger down Maddie's cheek and planting a kiss on her temple before holding out his hand. "Her timing is impeccable."

"It always is. I suppose we should go

in." Maddie took his hand and starting toward the parlor.

"Wait." Thomas pulled her back to him and wrapped her in his arms once more. "There is something I want to ask you first."

She sighed contentedly, breathing in the faint scent of the leather-bound books and ink he'd been using earlier in the day. "Ask me whatever you want. The answer is likely going to be yes."

"Will you marry me?" he returned softly.

Maddie's heart kicked into a gallop. Whatever she'd been expecting, it wasn't that. Not yet. "Are you sure?"

She knew his answer, of course—if there hadn't been a question of money, they'd probably already be wed. But there *was* a question of money, and she knew tutoring didn't bring in a large sum even when it was combined with her wages from Gran.

"Kit has offered us the old cottage on

his property for as long as we want it," Thomas explained. "With that, our savings, and your dowry, we should be comfortable. Not wealthy, but comfortable."

"The old cottage?" She reached back into her memory but couldn't recall anything.

"Downstream from where we used to fish. The structure is sound, and there's room for a small kitchen garden outside. Kit said he'd have the inside cleaned for us, and you can put your new sewing skills to work making curtains and things."

Maddie tried but failed to suppress a giggle. Gran had been trying to teach her how to run a household, and had included lessons in cooking and sewing in her curriculum. The cooking had been going well—their dinner that evening was her biggest test so far—but she'd not taken to sewing quite as well.

"I'm sure I could manage...eventually," she murmured with a half-smile. "But what about Gran? You know I want to marry you,

Thomas, but I can't leave her all alone."

"I've thought of that," he grinned, rubbing slow tracks up and down her back. "You could continue to be your grandmother's companion by day, and come home to me and our cottage in the evenings. Or, if you'd prefer to remain living here, perhaps your Gran will allow me to live here as well. I can give lessons from here as easily as I can from Kit's home."

Maddie tried to picture waking up beside Thomas every morning in the chamber she'd been given here in her grandmother's house and ended up giggling again.

"We don't have to decide now," he continued.

"Thank you," she said softly, smoothing back an auburn curl that had escaped his attempts to tame it.

"For what?"

"For giving me—us—options."

He smiled. "It really is more enjoyable

when we decide on things together."

She gave a low laugh. The day they'd worked out their current arrangements had included a spirited discussion...and was followed by another late night in front of the fireplace. *That* had certainly been enjoyable.

But the decision making had been pleasurable, too, if in a different way. They'd been able to really talk to one another, to share hopes and make plans for a small part of the future. "Yes," she replied softly.

"Wait—'yes' it was enjoyable, or..."

She went up on her toes and whispered in his ear, "Yes, I will marry you."

He sucked in a breath, then lifted her off her feet and swung her around in a full circle. "Sweeter words I'll never hear," he grinned, setting her down. His lips found hers, his mouth opening over hers as he deepened the kiss.

Someone cleared their throat nearby, about a second before Maddie lost all her inhibitions right there in Gran's entryway. With great reluctance, she disentangled herself from Thomas and turned to see who it was.

"I'm sorry to interrupt," Kit said in a half-whisper, gesturing toward the parlor. "It was either me or her."

Thomas laughed. "Thank God for small favors, then."

"Are we to have a new addition to the family, then?" Kit grinned.

"There are still some things to be decided," Maddie said, clasping her hands together in utter happiness. "But yes."

"Wonderful!" Kit practically bellowed. Then, in a quieter voice he continued, "You've been my sister in all but name since we were children. Now it will be official."

Thomas reached for Maddie. "Could you go make our excuses for just another moment, brother? There is one more thing I would like to say to my betrothed." He waited until Kit had disappeared down the hallway before encircling Maddie in his arms.

"What is it that can't wait?" she asked, hearing the trepidation in her own voice.

"I love you."

His voice was low and full of emotion, and her heart fluttered in response. She slipped her arms around his neck and bowed her head against his chest, hoping to hide the tears that sprung unexpectedly to her eyes.

When she could trust herself again, she turned her head and whispered, "I love you, too."

For that moment, it was just the two of them in each other's arms and all was right with the world.

Then Maddie sighed. "We should probably go in."

"How do you think your Gran will take the news?" Thomas asked, releasing his hold on her body in exchange for holding her hand.

"She'll be happy because we're happy,"

Maddie replied with a smile.

"Will she be disappointed that I'm not Kit?"

Maddie clasped his hand to her heart. "There's no way she could have watched me with you these past months and think that I would want to be with anyone else."

Thomas palmed her cheek and pressed a gentle kiss to her lips. "Then your plan worked," he smiled. "We've finally convinced someone that you don't want to marry Kit."

"Ah, but the most important people knew it all along." She looked deep into his blue eyes, then kissed him one more time. "Now let's go tell everyone else."

Ready for more Maitland Maidens? Read on for a sneak peek...

A Kiss to Build a Dream On

Maitland Maidens Book 4

Chapter 1

The Cotswolds
July 1815

Margaret Maitland sat at her brother's dining table, as she did at least once every week, wondering how she got to this point and where she was going from here.

Not literally how she got there—she walked from the dower house, as usual—but she'd had a letter from her son, Alex, earlier in the day which sent a contemplative wave washing over her. He'd been so small when they'd first moved into that house, and she'd been so vulnerable.

But he was a tall, strapping lad now, looking forward to the end of the Easter Term at Cambridge when he could come home and have some fun. Where had the time gone?

"Margaret?"

Margaret's brother Philip, seated next to her, poked her discreetly under the table. "Hmm?" she asked, turning her head toward the sound of her name.

Philip's wife Adeleine frowned across the table and set down her knife with a clank. "I asked if you and Alexander would be attending Natalie's practice ball."

"Yes, of course we will," Margaret answered readily. Adeleine had been hosting a series of informal events over the past several months to give her daughter the opportunity to practice being out in society before her first season in London. Only family and close friends had been invited thus far, but this "practice ball," as Adeleine had been calling it, would be something of a larger affair.

Adeleine's face relaxed and she sat back a bit in her chair. "Good. Natalie has been looking forward to dancing with her cousin."

Margaret chuckled, and Mr. Stephen Eddington, the Maitlands' neighbor sitting across the table from her, lifted a sandy eyebrow in inquiry. "When she was still in leading strings, Natalie decided that Alex was her favorite person in the world, and she's never wavered from that opinion."

"Ah," Mr. Eddington replied with a smile and a nod. "And Alex must return the sentiment, given how much my nephew Patrick includes her in his letters."

Adeleine glanced from Mr. Eddington to her husband, a range of emotions playing out on her face. When outrage made an appearance, Margaret caught Adeleine's eye and shook her head slightly.

"Mr. Eddington's nephew is Alex's closest friend," Margaret reminded her gently. "It's natural that they would speak to each other of the people they care for."

"Yes, that is it exactly," Mr. Eddington added. "Patrick says he feels as if he knows Miss Natalie because Alex speaks of her so often, and so highly."

Adeleine's eyes bored into Margaret's for a long moment. Margaret could practically see her sister-in-law's thoughts —she was afraid her daughter was going to be ruined before she even had a single season. Like her aunt.

Though, to be fair, Margaret had enjoyed three seasons before she had been ruined.

Adeleine nodded faintly, then smiled brightly at Mr. Eddington. "That is good to hear. And oh! Perhaps you would consider attending Natalie's practice ball as well? It will be held right here in our music room in a month's time."

"I would be honored," he replied, his hand going to his chest. "And on the subject of invitations, I came to dinner tonight with my own." His blue eyes slid from Adeleine to Margaret, and a small smile formed on his lips.

"Oh?" Margaret said, taking a sip of sweet red wine, the tide of her contemplation ebbing as a warmer wave washed in.

He grinned, then stifled the expression and cleared his throat. "For all of you. My sister and her children are coming to stay with me for several weeks, and I was hoping to persuade the three of you, along with Miss Natalie and Alex, to join us."

"Like a house party?" Margaret asked, carefully setting her glass on the table.

"A small one," Mr. Eddington acknowledged. "It would just be our two families. I've written to my friend James Fitzsimmons and your cousin Lady Cecilia to invite them as well, but I believe they are otherwise occupied."

Margaret grinned, slicing her roasted chicken and savoring the salty, meaty aroma. Cecilia had recently wed Mr. Fitzsimmons in what was supposed to be a marriage of convenience, but it had turned into a genuine love match. They were spending the summer visiting family and enjoying their new life together.

"My sister has five children, and the oldest girl is about Miss Natalie's age," Mr. Eddington continued over the clinking of silverware against plates. "Since Alex is already friends with my eldest nephew, we thought perhaps the younger ones would enjoy spending some time together while we of a certain age enjoy each other's company."

"That sounds like a capital idea," Philip said, brandishing his fork with enthusiasm. "I don't believe we'll be able to stay, not with all the preparations we must make before we travel to London after the practice ball. But your home is an easy ride, particularly when the weather is fine, and we may be able to join you some days."

Adeleine was smiling as well, but the warmth had begun to seep out of Margaret's body. "I- I'm not sure—"

"My sister has asked for you especially,

Miss Maitland," Mr. Eddington replied before she could finish her thought, his voice softer now as he pinned Margaret with his gaze once again. "She wants to meet the mother of her son's best friend."

"Oh, of– of course... And I would be pleased to meet her as well..."

Mr. Eddington smiled broadly. If he heard the hesitation in Margaret's voice, he ignored it. "Wonderful! My sister will be the hostess, of course, and she'll send round the details when she arrives next week."

He turned back to his plate, fairly beaming at his food and, alternately, his companions for the duration of the meal. Margaret found the previously delicious fare chewy and tasteless, and only picked at her entree until they left the table for the drawing room. She tried to focus on the conversations going on around her, but had no luck there either.

When finally Mr. Eddington decided to return home, Margaret jumped up from her chair. "I should also take my leave."

"I'll see you to the gate if I may," he replied, catching her eye.

Margaret nodded her assent. This was their custom if they both happened to be dining with Philip and Adeleine, and it was interesting that he still asked after nearly a year of acquaintance rather than just assuming.

What was he going to say when she refused his invitation?

Neither of them spoke as they made their way through the house and out onto the long drive awash in the reds and oranges of the setting sun. But three steps from the house, she couldn't keep it in any longer.

"Mr. Eddington, are you certain about inviting me to your home, to meet your sister?" she asked, laying a hand on his arm to stop him. A lone songbird serenaded them from a nearby tree as if he had no cares in the world.

"Of course I am," he replied quickly. His

brows crowded down low over his eyes. "Why would you ask me that?"

She pressed her lips together, trying to discern just the right words to convey the absolute inappropriateness of her presence in a respectable home. "You know that I raised my son without the help of his father."

Mr. Eddington nodded slowly. "Yes."

"And you also know why."

He nodded again, glancing at her feet for a moment before meeting her eyes once again. Not long after they first met, Margaret had outlined the bare bones of the story—how she had become pregnant without being married and, rather than hide her condition and give the baby to another family to raise, she had elected to keep him, to raise him herself.

It had destroyed her reputation, of course. And though there were a select few people who would now receive her privately in their homes all these years later, Margaret was still not welcome at even the most obscure society functions.

Margaret's voice was rough when she spoke again. "I truly would like to meet your sister, but I am afraid that even after twenty years my reputation would tarnish hers."

"And, in turn, my nieces' reputations as well," he added quietly.

Margaret turned and began to walk down the drive, clasping her hands together behind her back to keep from taking his arm as she often did. She wanted to, but it didn't feel like the right thing to do at this moment. "Exactly so."

"What about your own niece?" he asked, falling into step beside her. He, too, refrained from touching her, which was both a relief and a disappointment somehow. "Does she not suffer from your connection?"

"It's easier for people to overlook a rogue family member when the Duke of Alston is her cousin."

"Mmm. I suppose it's the same for your

son as well."

She kicked a small rock to the side. "The stigma is a bit less because he's a man, but yes. Influential relatives outweigh a fallen mother for him some of the time."

They walked along in silence down the length of the drive, accompanied only by the rhythmic crunching of gravel beneath their feet, and Margaret felt some of the tension in her shoulders easing. She feared that she would have to explain to him the details of her situation to make him understand how bad it had been for the family and friends that had supported her, that still supported her.

But he didn't protest any further. When they arrived at the gate, he tipped his hat to her as he always did and held the gate open for her to pass through.

"Good evening, Miss Maitland," he said. His voice was even, and he met her eyes, so perhaps there were no hard feelings.

"Good evening, Mr. Eddington."

A week later later, Stephen rode back to Philip Maitland's home, Eastwood Manor, with two things in his saddle bag: his copy of *Observations on the Theory and Practice of Landscape Gardening* that he'd promised to lend to Philip, and a note for Miss Margaret Maitland from his sister, who was more than a little disappointed to hear that Miss Maitland had turned down the house party invitation.

Hopefully, both things would be well received.

"Eddington—what a nice surprise," Philip said, rising as Stephen was shown into the library by the Maitlands' butler. "Adeleine was wondering earlier about your house party activities, and here you are to ask."

"Ah yes," Stephen replied, taking his usual seat in a sturdy walnut chair. "My sister arrived yesterday with her children, and she is writing up a list. Everything is to be rather informal, but she'll send the details round when she's sorted it all out."

"Excellent," Philip answered, taking his own seat in a chair that had begun its life as the twin of Stephen's but had seen much more wear. "You must thank her for thinking of us, and of Natalie in particular."

"I will do that." Stephen fished around in his inner coat pocket and came up with the note he'd been tasked with delivering. "She also sent along a note for your own sister. Will you pass it along to her the next time she's here?"

Philip waved the note away. "You can give it to her yourself before you depart. She's with Adeleine now walking in the gardens, but they should be returning soon for luncheon."

"Oh." Well, that was unexpected. Though Stephen supposed it shouldn't be— Miss Maitland was frequently here when he was. "Well, that's perfect timing, then. Perhaps I can take an answer home with me today."

Their conversation drifted to other topics, including the book Stephen had brought, and an hour or so later Mrs. Maitland bustled in with a bright smile for her husband.

"I hope you're hungry," she said, touching his shoulder lightly. "Our cook has been experimenting with some new recipes, and there's a mountain of food. You'll stay and taste them all, won't you Mr. Eddington?"

Stephen pulled his gold pocket watch from the custom pocket in his waistcoat. "I'm afraid I cannot, Mrs. Maitland," he answered with real regret. The Maitlands' cook always created the most delicious dishes. "I promised my sister that I would help her with a few things this afternoon. I really only came by to give this note to your sister-in-law."

He produced the note again with Miss Maitland's name written in flowing script on the outside, and Mrs. Maitland nodded.

"Margaret stayed a few more minutes

in the garden nearest the house. You can deliver your sister's note to her there if you'd like."

Wonderful—perhaps she could spare a moment to speak with him, too, away from any listening ears. "I believe I will do that. Thank you," Stephen said with a little bow to Mrs. Maitland. "Thank you both."

Eastwood Manor wasn't overly large by aristocratic standards, and he found Miss Maitland with little trouble. She was seemingly lost in thought, admiring a stone statue that appeared to be of a roe deer as the wind tousled the curly brown hair that had managed to escape her bonnet, and Stephen cleared his throat.

"Oh, Mr. Eddington," she said, turning quickly toward him. "What a lovely surprise."

He tried desperately not to react, but he couldn't help the grin that spread across his face. He was a lovely surprise, was he?

"I am here mostly on behalf of my sister," he said, handing her the note

Caroline had written. "She would like you to reconsider your attendance at her house party."

Miss Maitland accepted the note and took several moments to read it over. Then her hazel eyes met his. "Do you know what this says?"

Stephen shook his head, shifting his weight from one foot to the other. "Caroline didn't tell me exactly, only that she was disappointed you declined her invitation."

"She talks about how I can't ruin her reputation, how she's the daughter of a master builder married to the fifth son of an inconsequential gentleman, and no one in society even knows she exists," Miss Maitland explained.

"That is all true," Stephen replied, clasping his hands behind his back just to get them out of his way. "One or two society folks may know she exists, as they are aware I have a sister. But she has no dealings with them."

"I see." Miss Maitland's gaze traveled back to the note as a stiff breeze blew through, and she grasped firmly with both hands. "She also says that she would very much appreciate my company and that of my son."

Stephen nodded, even though she wasn't looking at him. "Caroline has been looking forward to having another woman of a similar age to talk to. And Patrick has been making lists of all the things he wants to show your son while they are here together."

Miss Maitland met his eyes again with a small smile. "Alex may go, of course, and stay until you tire of him."

"And you?" Her mouth turned down and Stephen quickly added, "If you don't feel comfortable staying at my home, you're welcome to come for as many or as few activities as you'd like, or to not come at all. The decision is yours to make."

She pressed her lips together as her eyes searched his face. Even the birds seemed to hold their collective breath, quietly waiting for her answer.

After a long moment, she exhaled slowly. "Might I have a day to think it over?"

"Yes, of course. But don't place more importance on this party than it warrants." He resisted the urge to reach out and touch her, though for some reason it took considerable willpower. "The point of this house party is for our two families to enjoy each others' company for a while, to enjoy having Patrick and Alex with us, and that's all. If that sounds like a pleasant way to spend your time, come. If it doesn't, we will see each other another time."

He was mentally berating himself for adding the last part—perhaps she didn't care if she saw him again—when she smiled faintly. It could have been his imagination, for it was gone as quickly as it appeared, but Stephen didn't think so.

"All right," she said, her voice maddeningly neutral. "I will be here tomorrow helping Adeleine and Natalie prepare for Natalie's next outing. If our paths don't cross, I'll send a note with a footman to your home."

They said their goodbyes and Stephen made his way back to the Maitland stables for his horse. Would she attend? Would she stay in his home?

Stephen couldn't come up with a believable reason to visit Philip Maitland again the next day, so he remained at home, catching up with his sister, playing games with his nieces and nephews, trying not to listen for a knock at the door.

When a footman in Maitland livery did finally arrive, Stephen's stomach did a little flip as he accepted the note with his name printed neatly upon it.

Dear Mr. Eddington,

On behalf of my son and myself, I thank you and your sister for the invitation to your house party. We are both pleased to attend for the duration. If your sister needs any help making

arrangements, I am happy to assist her.
Margaret Maitland

"Caroline! She's coming!"

Caroline was at the front door with him a few moments later, clapping her hands together. "Wonderful! I'm so glad she changed her mind."

"I am too," he answered, scanning the note again.

He wasn't quite sure when it had happened, but sometime in the recent past Stephen had resolved to get to know Miss Maitland better. He was her brother's friend, after all, and they met often at Eastwood Manor.

Perhaps this house party was their chance to develop a relationship independent of their mutual connection.

Other Books by Cora Lee

Sweet & Traditional:
Save the Last Dance for Me (Maitland Maidens #1)
Back In My Arms Again (Maitland Maidens #2)
Kissing by the Mistletoe (Maitland Maidens #3)
A Kiss to Build a Dream On (Maitland Maidens #4)
When I Fall In Love (Maitland Maidens #5)

Spicy Novellas:
What If I Loved You

Spicy and Suspenseful:
No Rest for the Wicked
The Good, The Bad, And The Scandalous
The Duke of Darkness

About the Author

Cora Lee is a National Bestselling author of Regency romance. She went on a twelve year expedition through the blackboard jungle as a high school math teacher before publishing *Save the Last Dance for Me*, the first book in the Maitland Maidens series. She then followed it up with eight more novels and novellas ranging from sweet and traditional to spicy and suspenseful.

When she's not walking Rotten Row at the fashionable hour or attending the entertainments of the Season, you might find her participating in Romance Writers of America events, wading through her towering TBR pile, or eagerly awaiting the next Marvel movie release. If you'd like to find out more about Cora or her books you can visit her website, sign up for her newsletter, or connect with her on Bookbub, Facebook, or Goodreads.